LOVING YOU WAS MY UNDOING

JAVIER GONZALEZ–RUBIO

translated by
Yareli Arizmendi and Stephen Lytle

A John Macrae Book

Henry Holt and Company   New York

Henry Holt and Company, Inc.
Publishers since 1866
115 West 18th Street
New York, New York 10011

Henry Holt® is a registered trademark of
Henry Holt and Company, Inc.

Library of Congress Cataloging-in-Publication Data
González-Rubio, Javier.
[Quererte fue mi castigo. English]
Loving You Was My Undoing / Javier González-Rubio ;
translated by Yareli
Arizmendi and Stephen Lytle.—1st ed.
p.   cm.
"A John Macrae book."
ISBN 0-8050-4878-2 (alk. paper)
I. Arizmendi, Yareli.   II. Lytle, Stephen.   III. Title.
PQ7298.17.0515Q4713   1999
863—dc21   98-5712

Henry Holt books are available for special promotions and premiums.
For details contact: Director, Special Markets.

First Edition 1998

Designed by Paula Russell Szafranski

Printed in the United States of America
All first editions are printed on acid-free paper. ∞

1   3   5   7   9   10   8   6   4   2

LOVING YOU
WAS MY UNDOING

ONE

NO ONE COULD HAVE IMAGINED THAT THE MEXICAN REVO-
lution would pass through Monreal. And it never would have
if it hadn't been for a motley bunch of federal soldiers who
were fleeing defeat and certain death at the hands of the revolutionaries at the battle of Alamilla.

In the quiet afternoon there was no reason to suspect that
by nightfall the bells of Santa María del Refugio would be
wailing like widows over the dead because of a minor skirmish
of no real significance to the Revolution. But the action did
allow Federico Farías to dream of becoming a hero.

On the other hand, the taking of Alamilla was a memorable
battle, the result of a tactical alliance between two cunning
young generals: Valentín Cobelo, a loner from the desert, and
Francisco Larios, a loyal servant of the revolution.

They had met a few days earlier at the Hacienda La Quintilla amidst Belgian tapestries, Spanish ironwork, ebony, mahogany, and marble, Bohemian crystal, Limoges and Sèvres porcelain, Austrian candelabra. The hacienda had become General Larios's headquarters shortly after its owners, the Acevedo Rincón family, fled to Houston with their money and jewels, fearing a surprise visit from the infamous Pancho Villa. Don Jesús Acevedo had been a rancher, an apple and peach farmer, and a budding steel magnate.

General Larios was a true *revolucionario:* he knew what he was fighting for and why. Moreover, he enjoyed the complete confidence of his superior, General Felipe Angeles, both men sharing a common military strategy and recognizing the importance of clemency. Various details about Valentín Cobelo's prowess had reached Larios, and these left no doubt as to the man's ferocity in battle. But what of his ideals? Larios arrogantly promised an alliance between the two willful men to bolster the ranks of the revolutionary army's northern division.

That day in La Quintilla the generals sat facing each other across the hacienda's immense colonial dining table. Set before each man were a glass and a bottle of cognac, which had been liberated from Don Jesús' wine cellar.

Cobelo was accompanied by his right-hand man Cipriano, his first lieutenant Serafín Machuca, and Baltasar Juan, a Tarahumara Indian known as Rarámuri. Not far off, under the charge of Julián Vela, Cobelo's five hundred men waited.

Serafín Machuca and Cipriano sat behind Cobelo, staring at the floor and concentrating on every word. Rarámuri leaned against a window framed by silk brocade curtains, a sheathed machete slung over his left shoulder; two knives were visible at his waist below the twin bandoliers displayed across his chest. He held his Winchester by the barrel, its stock firmly planted on the floor. Five of Larios's men were positioned close by, within earshot of the conversation between the two generals.

Beginning the dialogue was difficult. As Larios struggled to find the best way of presenting his ideas to Cobelo, he found himself up against the impenetrable barrier of the general's austere courtesy. And his fixed stare, which seemed that of a man whom death had surprised and left with open eyes.

Larios began the conversation by mentioning General Felipe Angeles, relying on his superior's character and reputation to attract a true revolucionario.

"I know General Angeles would be pleased to meet you. He has great respect for honorable men. He recognizes them right away and realizes their value to the *revolución*. He is a true general"—Larios attempted a smile—"a brigadier, no less. He hasn't been with General Villa long; he was with Carranza before, that pompous old ass." He smiled more broadly this time, expecting a similar reaction from Valentín Cobelo.

Cobelo remained unmoved. There was a pause. Larios stretched in his chair and decided to go right to the point.

"I want you to help me take Alamilla. Don't misunderstand me. I'm not after the glory. We'll each command our own men, but we'll attack together. Once we have united, our only orders will come from General Angeles or General Villa himself. What do you think?"

"No."

The two men stared at each other. Larios pushed back and straightened his legs, trying not to show his aggravation.

"I have three thousand men, all well armed and loyal," he added, in an attempt to fill the silence.

Cobelo stared at him, as if the words meant nothing. This was probably true.

"You go your own way, drifting, and one of these days you'll disappear. Somebody will kill you. That would be such a waste, so irresponsible." Larios paused. "I say this with all due respect, General Cobelo. We have to finish off Huerta and those other bastards." He took out a cigarette and felt around in his jacket for a match.

"Then what?" asked Cobelo, as he pulled a cigar from an inner pocket of his brown suede jacket.

"What do you mean, 'Then what?' " Larios handed Cobelo the matches.

An ironic smile played across the other man's face, which Larios took as a gesture of thanks. "After Huerta is finished, and Carranza . . . and the revolución."

Larios sighed deeply and tightened his jaw.

Rarámuri moved slightly away from the window. He cradled his rifle in his arms and looked at the generals.

"We'll build a new country, make new laws, live in peace," Larios said.

"Revolutions never end when or how people want them to, General Larios. Villa, Angeles, even you—who do you think will still be alive when it's over?" Cobelo blew out a cloud of smoke and took a sip of cognac.

"What do you want?" In his anger, Larios crushed his cigarette in the porcelain ashtray.

"To fight, General." Valentín was cool and precise. "To take what I want and leave the rest. To escape death as long as I can. That's enough for me."

It was not the response Larios had expected. He sat up in his chair, and his men took a few steps forward. They did not think much of this Valentín Cobelo.

6

Measuring them with his eyes, Rarámuri straightened up too. Certain that Larios had made a mistake, Cipriano and Serafín were also alert. What mattered here was capturing Alamilla. Another misjudgment by Larios would eliminate all possibility of that victory. Cipriano, however, felt instinctively that, in spite of everything, his boss considered this Larios a decent man.

"You don't believe in the revolution or anything else." Larios sounded more deceived than judgmental.

Serafín Machuca lifted his hat from his head, ran a hand over his hair, and replaced the hat.

Cobelo stood up, placed his hands on the table, and spoke. "Look, I don't like answering questions. You want me to help you at Alamilla? I will. But that's it. I don't take orders from anyone, and I don't run around with anybody. You do what you have to do, and I'll do what I have to do. Agreed?"

Although he took pains not to show it by word or appearance, Larios was greatly relieved. "Agreed."

"Now we're getting somewhere." Cobelo sat back down and refilled his glass with Don Jesús' cognac. He sensed from the silence that Larios was waiting for him to lay out a plan.

"We'll go in from the north the day after tomorrow, as soon as it gets dark."

"Go in from the desert?" said Larios incredulously, as he lit up another cigarette.

"It's the only way. Otherwise they'll crush us. I know the desert well. They'll never expect an attack from that side. We'll send four or five hundred of your men to use the other approaches, but most of us will go in from the north. It's only eight hours through the desert."

"Then, fresh as daisies, we attack?"

Cobelo was not amused by sarcasm. "No, I think we'd

be better off attacking as men. Daisies wouldn't stand a chance."

Larios smiled despite himself and focused on Cobelo's expressionless face. What thoughts lay behind that arid exterior? He gave up wondering and leaned back in his chair. "How do you come to know the desert so well, don Valentín?"

Cobelo stood, shrugged, and removed the cigar from his mouth. Behind him, Cipriano and Serafín also stood up, and Rarámuri took a few steps forward. "It's inside me, don Francisco, deep inside." He put the cigar back in his mouth and left with his men.

Two days later, as night began to fall on Alamilla, three hundred revolucionarios appeared just south of town. From General Sebastian Alcocer's vigilant troops, guarding the central plaza, a trumpet sounded an alarm, and a thousand federales hastily took up positions at the southern end of town and waited nervously for the revolucionarios to draw within firing range. As the men approached, they spread out over the vast terrain and began firing, even though the bullets fell far short of their marks. Alcocer observed the advancing troops with contempt, convinced that they were walking toward certain death.

Suddenly a shout came from the revolucionarios and they began running toward the village. Before long they were within range of the federales' artillery, now raining down upon them. After a number had fallen, they withdrew to a safe distance and regrouped before resuming their advance on the town. Alcocer could not believe that a few hundred men on foot expected to take Alamilla. He assumed it was a distraction and that the real attack was still to come, probably with horses and cannons. He ordered his men to stop firing and wait until the attackers came closer before firing again. As a precaution, he sent a hundred men north to guard the desert approach. But the revolucionarios never advanced close enough to draw fire. They stopped short, in full view of the impatient federales, until it was completely dark.

Meanwhile, the men General Alcocer had sent north were surprised by two thousand revolucionarios already galloping into town, guns blazing and machetes flashing. Scattering down the darkened streets, they tore doors off their hinges and threw flaming torches into windows. Villagers ran without knowing where to go. Some hid behind thick wooden doors until the doors were kicked in by the hooves of horses wild with confusion and fear. Columns of smoke rose in the streets, flames illuminating the revolucionarios as they destroyed Alamilla. Too late, General Alcocer, sweating with despair, tried to improvise a defense, but the cannons were too heavy and the maddening machine guns were massacring the townspeople. Cadavers were trampled by horses, then buried by newer casualties. Some horsemen fell, but not nearly as many as General Alcocer would have wanted, not enough to stop these men, who wielded their machetes better than the federales could handle their swords. Surrounded by death and dismembered bodies, the federal troops couldn't escape to the south because the other revolucionarios were still waiting, guns loaded and ready. Only a few dozen federales managed to escape the devastated pueblo.

In the village, women cringed in corners, praying in vain for mercy; only the children were spared, as they hid in cellars, listening to the clattering of horses' hooves, the slashing of machetes, gunfire and screams. Little by little the shots were replaced by laughter, crackling bonfires, stifled weeping and moaning. Rising above everything came the words to an old, nearly forgotten song: *Wanting you was my curse, God help me forget your love.*

Francisco Larios looked over the ruins of the town, contemplating the agony caused by his victory. He ordered his men not to shoot anyone else or plunder the goods of the living or rape the women. Then he made his way over to Valentín Cobelo. "We have won this town. Now it's ours."

Cobelo smiled amiably, without looking at Larios. "You can have it," he said. "A few federales escaped. I'll give them a head start so they'll think they got away."

"Aren't you ever afraid of losing?" Larios asked, a hint of admiration and disbelief registering in his voice.

The question took Valentín Cobelo back to his childhood. *Aren't you ever afraid of falling off the horse, Cipriano? I am,* he had confessed. *That's something you should never think about, boy; otherwise you will fall. Animals can smell fear; they use it to break you,* Cipriano had told him.

"Are *you* ever afraid, General?" asked Cobelo, remembering Cipriano's words.

"Yes, but I conquer my fears," replied Larios, with honest pride.

"If you can conquer them, save yourself the thought in the first place."

Two days later a man entered Monreal, galloping at full speed and yelling that a hundred ragged federales were approaching.

What the breathless rider didn't know was that the federales were speeding toward Monreal because General Valentín Cobelo was right behind them.

TWO

AT THIRTY-FOUR, FEDERICO FARIAS WAS THE NOTARY PUBLIC of Monreal. He drew up wills, sales contracts, land transfers, and sworn testimonies and was an official witness to legal documents. He also acted as an intellectual messenger for the revolution.

Farías had studied law at the University of Mexico in Mexico City. Before war had been declared against Porfirio Díaz, he arrived in Monreal with huge trunks and cases filled with an eclectic assortment of incendiary books and magazines.

After settling in and establishing his business, he devoted his free time to speaking about the political ideas behind the armed movement for justice and democracy. Later, with equal fervor, he embraced those born of the revolución itself.

Gradually the quiet people of Monreal—who enjoyed the new gatherings because stories about the leaders of the revolución were recounted and invented—learned how Farías had formed his political ideas.

They listened to him speak nostalgically of his attendance at the first Liberal Congress in San Luis Potosí when he was twenty-two. They heard him give an extensive explanation of his decision to join the Liberal Party. But even more detailed and convincing was the story of his decision to abandon that party and join the National Unification Party. Farías's speeches promoting don Francisco I. Madero were delivered with great solemnity. He had a carefully maintained and autographed copy of Madero's book, *The Presidential Succession,* which he delighted in showing to his listeners. Nevertheless, he was still able to convince his neighbors that the president had not managed to fulfill the demand for social justice that he had inspired. And thus he felt justified in persuading them to cast a vote in favor of Pascual Orozco's Cannery Plan. But never was his oratory power so evident as when he called a meeting to declare his praise for Madero, martyred by the traitorous and unworthy Victoriano Huerta. Farías's listeners also detected his shy admiration for Francisco Villa, who, emerging from the lowest rung of the ladder but possessed of a tenacious personality, had converted himself into a bold and aggressive rebel leader. Because information about Emiliano Zapata was scant, Federico Farías never mentioned him, and when someone brought him up, Farías would launch into a meandering discourse in an attempt to fend off questions. He had great admiration for the leaders who were shaping the country in these tortured times, and in speaking of their noble deeds he allowed his imagination to attribute to them words and actions that he would have liked to have said and done himself.

Federico Farías gave great importance to the family. His own people had paid for his studies with profits from their wheat mills and general store. Then they provided him with enough money to establish himself in Monreal without having to worry about the affluence of his clientele. He was also a strong supporter of workers' rights, so no one was surprised when he became a founding member of the Catholic Workers Circle, reaffirming his belief in the cooperation of all classes as necessary to achieving social justice. Farías was certain the country would grow strong under the shelter of a strong legal system. He was noble, kind, and completely without malice.

Federico Farías revered all national heroes and, once settled in Monreal, he applied himself to learning local history and reviving the memory of the illustrious don Lisandro López de Gandía. This Basque adventurer and gold miner, tired of sending back to Spain the immense wealth he found in the mines of Zacatecas, had decided to take to the road and, with a group of friends, assorted followers, and a few uprooted Indians, wandered north until arriving on May 6 in the Year of Our Lord 1692 at the present-day site of Monreal.

In the church of Santa María del Refugio, erected by don Lisandro and the resting place for his remains, Federico found a barely legible manuscript written by the Spaniard:

In the distance I saw a place so beautiful I thought it must be sacred. And when we arrived there, all of us tired of nothing but desert, we could do nothing but laugh and hug one another with happiness before such greenness as that which lay before our eyes and feet, reminding me of the countryside of my youth in the Basque country. I decided we would stay there to build our town, Monreal de Nuestra Señora del Refugio.

Everyone agreed we should remain just where the desert gave way to the lush green hills.

Federico arranged for the plans of the original town, which was not much changed, to be displayed in glass cabinets in the municipal building. There was one long street, now called Las Margaritas, with houses on both sides, some made of stone dragged from the hills and others of adobe. Most were only one story, but all had huge doors of heavy carved wood in the baroque style, covered with angels and flowers. By the time Federico arrived, many of these houses had been painted pink, blue, or white. Some had added porticoes with columns and steps in the French style—even Monreal felt the Parisian influence that had enraptured the followers of Porfirio Díaz in the capital—but few houses, like Federico's, which boasted two stories, retained the natural color of its stones. The windows were covered by wooden shutters that creaked and groaned on nights when the desert winds beat tirelessly against the little town on the hill.

The village had grown in an orderly and harmonious manner. By the end of the eighteenth century, there were two other streets parallel to Las Margaritas. The school and post office (with telegraph) were on one; the other featured specialty shops, the blacksmiths, and the cantina. It was a quiet town, with tall men and well-formed women, mestizos descended from don Lisandro and his friends. They had discovered the beauty and shape of the nearby Indian women, who were very different in appearance and height from those in the central and southern part of Nueva España.

Federico Farías reinstituted the tradition, lost over the years, of celebrating May 6 as the town's anniversary and organized civic ceremonies at the elementary school on the birthdays of national heroes. He helped the schoolchildren write essays about the country's martyrs and never allowed them to denigrate the character of Porfirio Díaz.

A sizable group of devoted followers appeared every Friday afternoon at the Café Las Palmas to hear him speak. It was there he always thought he would die, of natural causes—not like his fellow student Rutilio Argudín, stabbed to death in the doorway of his home during the liberal revolt of 1906. The pain and fear caused by the sight of the bloody corpse of a young man with his whole life in front of him had convinced Federico Farías that it was not necessary for him to remain in Mexico City in order to take part in the revolution. He was absolutely certain that he wanted to die an old man. He was afraid of the violence inherent in a noble battle and was terrified of jumping on a horse armed with a gun. Instead, he galloped from one political idea to another to prevent himself from betraying what he considered to be the essence of the revolution: the revolution itself.

Rosario Alomar, whom he married after living in Monreal for a year and a half, was the greatest source of his respect. She was the daughter of don Celestino Alomar, a Spaniard who left one day for Cuba to defend what was left of an empire upon which—it was said—the sun never set. The wandering adventurer had apparently died a hero on that faraway island.

Because of her incredible arrogance, and despite her indescribable and much-discussed beauty, Rosario Alomar's future as a lonely spinster had already been set in the minds of the townspeople.

Rosario's neighbors surmised that she had married Federico because of his respectability, education, and good manners. His air of urban sophistication was palpable, even though he was only from Torreón. Still, people were always saying—behind closed doors, of course—that he definitely wasn't man enough for such a woman. One of these days, they said, she would be carried away by a wealthy rancher like Efraín Gutiérrez, who, despite holding vastly differing views, demonstrated a keen interest in Federico's ideas and often visited him at home, sparking further gossip among Rosario's envious neighbors.

Before Federico had arrived, Efraín Gutiérrez, dignified yet persistent, had courted Rosario in vain. He silently endured her disdain but boasted of his courtship to the other young women in town. None but the most naive believed him. Meanwhile, charm boiled in his blood, waiting.

No one dared judge Federico or Rosario publicly. She inspired desire and envy; it wasn't respect that kept people silent, but fear of incurring the wrath of this hot-tempered daughter of Spain.

Once, coming out of mass, the Pintado sisters, dressed demurely in pink and carrying parasols, snickered maliciously as Rosario and Federico passed. When Rosario arrived at her carriage she let go of Federico's arm, took the horsewhip, and, to her husband's amazement, lashed the backs of the laughing sisters, knocking them to the ground.

"What are you idiots laughing at?" she asked.

The women were crying, unable to stand. They did not answer.

"Are you after Federico? Take him, then! He's right here. But you better do it now, or get out of here and find someone else!"

Shamed by the spectacle, the young women cried even harder.

Rosario was preparing to deliver another blow when her

husband held her arm. Fear of drawing Rosario's wrath himself prevented him from helping the sisters.

As soon as they arrived home, Federico reproached Rosario for her vulgar display and her use of force. It was one thing to act like that at home, another to do so in public. For him it had been an occasion of great shame, and he told her that she had damaged their reputation.

Doña Severina agreed with her son-in-law. Rosario should have ignored them, a couple of sniveling girls dying to get married.

Rosario listened in silence, peacefully eating her breakfast. "And on top of it all, after taking communion," added doña Severina.

A few minutes passed before Rosario spoke. "Look, Federico, those two are a pair of idiots. That wasn't the first time I've heard their stupid giggles. One protects honor and pride by defending them, and since I don't know how to make lofty speeches like you, I responded my way. You know who I am, and so does everyone else in this town. We all know what those two fools were laughing at. And don't worry." She turned to her mother. "I did not take communion today."

She stood up gracefully and began to clear the table. Federico watched her every move.

"She has spoken, señora," he said to doña Severina.

"What that girl needs is a good spanking."

"Well, I'm not going to do it," Federico told her. He walked up to Rosario as she washed the dishes and kissed her on the forehead. He looked at her lovingly, admiringly. She gazed back tenderly. Then he went to the post office to see if any magazines had arrived from the capital.

Doña Severina entered the kitchen. "That man truly loves you. It's just too bad he's not man enough to handle you."

"Mamá, you're always saying that. I prefer him to all those pompous, macho imbeciles who proclaim their virility and end up losing everything to their wonderful revolución."

"Ay, *hija*, how you talk." With Rosario's hands still in the soapy water, doña Severina ventured, "That Efraín looks like a nice enough man, but there's something about him that makes me uneasy. You just concentrate on Federico. That's what your father would say."

Rosario tightened her grip on the plate she was rinsing and looked her mother straight in the eye. "I've got enough on my mind just thinking about you and me, so don't talk to me about how things would be different if my father were still alive. I married Federico because I wanted to. Let's leave it at that."

Federico was napping under a hot, sleepy sun when Jorge Quintero, anxious and gasping for breath, arrived to report that fifty or sixty federales were approaching Monreal on horseback. It was unbelievable, inconceivable. As Rosario heard the news, she felt the walls crack.

"Where are they coming from? Who saw them?" Federico began praying to himself to keep calm.

"I think they'll cross the river at the ford. A kid came running into town to tell us," answered Jorge, anxiously awaiting instructions from his leader.

Federico turned his back to his friend. Trembling and unsure, he stroked his beard. His hands were sweaty and his heart beat furiously in his chest. Without fanfare, the revolution with all its brutality had found Monreal. Maybe it was just passing by, he thought. He had nothing to fight with, but maybe that didn't really matter, since the soldiers had already been defeated at Alamilla.

"What are we going to do?" asked Jorge, barely containing

his impatience. He needed a clear, firm order, one worthy of a revolutionary.

"Notify everyone in the circle to meet at the municipal building," said Federico, just to say something, and Quintero ran off, sombrero in hand, full of naive enthusiasm.

Federico knew what Jorge and the others expected from him. He was afraid to leave, afraid to stay home. Not knowing where to turn, he choked in claustrophobic anguish. It was Rosario who opened the door for him.

"Take this. You can't let them in the gates." She handed him an old hunting rifle that had belonged to don Celestino.

Federico Farías hesitated. It had all been in vain. No speech, no homage, no adulation or tribute could have prevented this moment from arriving. The look in Rosario's eyes sparked his courage and filled him with the illusion of bravery. He grabbed the rifle and went out into the street, thinking that later in the afternoon his neighbors would applaud his actions. Perhaps his name, uttered with respect and admiration, would reach ears in Mexico City. After all, there weren't that many federales heading their way, and surely they were tired and hungry, possibly even unarmed.

"Why did you do that?" doña Severina asked her daughter reproachfully.

"I did it to save him from his own shame. Isn't that what my father did when he went to Cuba?"

"He never came back."

"Who asked them to be men?"

"You're a cold woman, Rosario."

"Do you think that after everything Federico has said in this town they would still respect him if he didn't confront those federales? He would bring shame on all of us, especially me. And I did not marry him to be humiliated."

Thirty men with ancient rifles and pistols had already gathered when Federico arrived at the municipal building. The municipal president, his friend and sympathizer, tried unconvincingly to dissuade him. "Surely they just want to rest and eat something; then they'll be on their way," he assured Federico. Everyone else was in favor of contributing to the revolution. Since these were government soldiers, they were enemies. One man suggested they ask them to surrender, then incarcerate them until the disruption blew over, but he found no support. "We're men enough to give them their due," the others said. Thrilled that so many men had absorbed his teaching, Federico took advantage of his oratorical skill to exalt this opportunity of gaining a place in the annals of history. He was reminded of the defense of the Alamo by the army of Santa Anna, but he couldn't think of a way to make the comparison. So instead he mentioned the siege of Cuautla, which left no doubt what had to be done: launch a worthy attack on these thieves, these degenerates, these enemies of democracy.

As the men walked along Margaritas, the town's main street, toward the entrance to town, they shouted that all houses should be shuttered and no one should come out until further notice. Young girls sighed excitedly as they passed, and several young boys—not even twenty yet—joined them, feigning gallantry and eager to participate in a battle like the ones their grandfathers had mounted against the Apaches.

The thirty revolutionaries took up positions behind columns, in spaces between buildings, on roofs. They blocked the road with a couple of carriages and drenched them with gasoline so they could torch them if the federales got too close. The streets were empty. Some of the women began to chant novenas and sing hymns. Rosario Alomar, with faint but sincere hope, entrusted the men to God. Nowhere was even the faintest sound heard or movement perceived. The quiet became suffocating.

The federales being pursued by Valentín Cobelo approached at a wild gallop. There were no more than fifty of them, enveloped in a cloud of yellow dust and exhaustion. Nervous and anxious, Federico's men began shooting before they were within range. Faced with the unpleasant alternatives of retracing their steps and confronting Cobelo and his men or changing direction and heading for the open desert, the soldiers spread out and charged directly at the town. The men of Monreal lost precious time as they reloaded their weapons.

The federales' bullets set fire to the gasoline-soaked carriages, and the men positioned behind them fled, trousers aflame. The federales kept firing, and a dozen or so urged their horses over the burning carriages, hooves and bellies scorched by the flames. The rest followed and searched out their attackers, finding and shooting them behind columns and on the roofs. Bodies tumbled to the ground.

Valentín Cobelo's men drew near. A geyser of sweat poured down Federico's face, mingling with his tears and hampering his ability to see and aim with the accuracy he desperately sought. The federales weren't falling. They seemed to be everywhere. And worse, something he had never even considered, those townspeople who were supporters of the federal government, among whom was Efraín Gutiérrez, more from self-promotional than courageous motives, had taken to the streets and were shooting at their neighbors who were shooting at the federales. Terrified, Federico decided to surrender, to call out for everyone to stop shooting. It was senseless to kill each other like this. So he walked out of his hiding place, careful not to step on Jorge Quintero's lifeless body, and was immediately hit with dozens of stray bullets. As he collapsed in a puddle of his own blood, a soldier stuck a sword in his belly.

In all the confusion, Efraín Gutiérrez, without having fired a single shot, glanced disdainfully at Federico's body and slipped away, firm in his belief that his life and hacienda were worth more than these suicidal fools. The soldiers started shooting at the townspeople who had joined them. They took up positions to defend themselves from Cobelo's men, who now descended upon them, their machetes slicing the heat. Knives flew at throats that never uttered a final scream. Bones were crushed by machete-wielding men who had never before walked these worn cobblestones. And death, like no one could ever have imagined, made its way into the houses lining the quiet old street, now defenseless and paralyzed, forced to witness its gutters flow with blood.

Waving his machete like a flag, Valentín Cobelo spun around on his horse, calling out orders. He glimpsed the commander of the federales and spurred his horse down Margaritas after him. Sensing danger, the officer turned around and, seeing the crazed figure of Cobelo approaching, tried to run faster, but the circling machete traced a half moon around his shoulder, slicing his arm from its socket. Horror, more than pain, made him fall to the ground. And then reflex made him stand again before his other arm was severed in a similar fashion. Cobelo stopped his horse and turned to watch what remained of the man, twisting and dancing, as if the torrents of blood from his sockets were all that kept him from falling.

Just then Cobelo saw a carriage approaching, drawn by two reckless horses. Armed only with blind courage, anger, and a horsewhip, the woman driving the carriage saw the nightmarish figure on horseback and continued on her way. She regretted not having a pistol in her hand when the man brusquely left his latest victim, rode over, leaned forward, and grabbed the bridle of her terrified mares. In vain she whipped her horses; he held on, attempting to change the direction of the carriage while she struck at him with the whip and ordered him to let go and let her continue on her way. When he finally managed to turn the mares, he saw in her tense, open face and eyes all that she was in that instant: fury, pain, and beauty. Like an eagle approaching its prey, he circled her. She straightened in her seat and clenched her teeth, aware of the short distance separating her from those sharp eyes. He was still not ready to descend and seize her.

No one who had known Valentín Cobelo would have believed his eyes could sparkle with such brilliance. He watched his majestic prey launching her attack with the desperation of a caged beast. Valentín wrapped the stinging whip around his hand and gave it such a pull that Rosario nearly lost her balance, but her pride helped her not to fall and show defeat. He threw the whip aside and began stroking the head of the nearer mare, his eyes never leaving the woman who had bewitched him.

"Get out of here," he ordered.

"My husband is over there," Rosario responded, full of self-confidence.

"That changes nothing. Get away from here. If you keep going in that direction you are likely to meet death. I give you my word that I'll send him to you as soon as I find him. What is your husband's name?"

"Federico Farías!" Rosario threw the name in his face.

Valentín moved aside and poked one of the mares. They took off at a full gallop in the same direction from which they had come. He returned to the fray and ordered his men to stop.

Cipriano stared at the rider who was one with his horse in the middle of the slaughtered lives of those not able to hold on to them.

"We'll sleep here tonight," ordered Valentín.

"What did you see, boy?" Cipriano asked.

"A woman, and I promised to return a dead man to her."

THREE

CHARIOTS OF GRAY CLOUDS PULLED BY THUNDER HORSES AP-
peared across the sky, carrying rain to Monreal. Barely notice-
able at first, the drizzle became a downpour, flooding the
land, the bodies, the blood, the sorrow.

The bells of Santa María del Refugio rang desolately.
Carried on the wind, the tolling dripped through the streets,
leaked under doors and windows, poured through the walls,
before disappearing into the desert.

The thirsty rain drank up all the colors. Approaching
nightfall held no hint of consolation for the mourners, and
the already faint light began to retreat as if afraid it too would
meet the same unforeseen fate that had befallen the townspeople. Gradually the town grew darker. Men and women

dressed in black. All the joy in the children's laughter had been silenced, their faces smudged with pain.

On Margaritas Street, the federales were a heap of bones. Passersby crossed themselves and hurried on, not even pausing long enough to decide whether or not to offer a prayer for their unfortunate souls.

The vestibule of Santa María del Refugio was blanketed by a row of corpses, fallen citizens of Monreal, killed in the skirmish. Valentín Cobelo had ordered them to be placed there. The only body missing was that of Federico Farías, struck down while attempting to overreach his potential, as Rosario Alomar said.

"What are we going to do with all these poor souls, Father?" asked the sacristan.

"Exactly what we would do with one, my son: bless them, pray for them, and bury them as soon as we can." The priest could offer no words to explain God's will, which at times like these was unfathomable.

Several of Valentín Cobelo's men guarded the church entryway.

"We can't let any of these bodies escape and upset the general," said one of the men, without a trace of humor in his voice.

The rest of Cobelo's men, the *cobelistas*, had spread out in small groups around town. They stayed close to their cooking fires and under overhangs to avoid the rain, which gave no sign of dying itself. It was cold, or maybe it was just the contrast from the desert heat that made it seem so. While they cooked their supper, the men halfheartedly sang old love songs: *If not for you, dear, my heart would never have known the pain that love can bear.*

"Why'd he make us put all those bodies in the church, Cipriano? I don't remember ever moving bodies that weren't ours," said Serafín Machuca, once all the corpses had been assembled at Santa María del Refugio.

"Think about it, Serafín. You should be able to figure him out by now without asking me."

"Don't tell me this is all about the body he made Julián and Jerónimo deliver to the widow."

"It's not about the body."

Julián Vela, Jerónimo Pastor, and three other men had taken the body of Federico Farías to Rosario Alomar's house. It lay in the back of the wagon, wrapped carefully in sheets so it wouldn't get wet.

Still wearing the white blouse and blue skirt she had worn that morning when she ran into Valentín Cobelo, Rosario opened the door.

Julián and Jerónimo exchanged quick looks of complicity, acknowledging her beauty and their boss's good taste, and removed their hats. Julián Vela spoke.

"My general sent us to bring you this man. Where do you want us to put him?"

Rosario looked at the two men without seeing them. Her mother stood beside her. Doña Severina's face conveyed the revulsion they both felt for these two weathered men, sinewy and tanned, standing there, rain trickling from their hair onto their chests.

Rosario Alomar descended the stairs and walked slowly toward the wagon. She climbed up on it, neither man daring to offer assistance. She gently moved the sheets away from his face. Her husband's eyes were open, still fixed upon his shattered dreams. Rosario gazed at him for a moment, as if to share a secret. She had liked this man, despite his perpetually adolescent face, his lack of strength and resolve. Instead of flowers, he used to bring her books of poetry and speak to her about history. Pride had never made a home in him. When he gazed at Rosario, joy spread from his eyes, brightening his entire face. Never giving in to shame, he proclaimed his inability to learn to ride horseback: "I have come to the conclusion that the horses have all gotten together and decided to throw me. Not one could ever resist the temptation, so we just agreed to respect each other, and we've gotten along very well ever since."

That afternoon long ago doña Severina had taken longer than usual to check on the cookies she was baking in the oven, and Federico had addressed Rosario with a formality more playful than stuffy. "If you will marry me, then I will do likewise and marry you. We will both try to find happiness without having to risk breaking a promise of eternal commitment, though I do admire such pledges in poetry." Rosario appreciated the absence of assurances and guarantees, the use of the word "both," and not having to give herself unconditionally—all, she felt, signs of true love—so she said yes.

Now no one could see her tears. She wiped the dirt from his cheeks, nose, and mouth. Doña Severina, still standing in the doorway, sobbed loudly. The men stood nearby, their heads bowed as if they cared. Rosario climbed down off the wagon and approached Julián Vela.

"All the others were taken to the church." It was a statement, not a question.

"Yes, ma'am." He kept his head bowed.

"Then we'll take him there too. Wait for me." She entered the house and returned with a cape and an umbrella. Her mother already had a heavy shawl wrapped around her.

Rosario climbed up on the wagon and took the reins. Jerónimo Pastor helped Severina up.

They started toward town, Cobelo's men walking behind the wagon. Doña Severina was still crying and could barely hold the umbrella. Without thinking about her dead husband lying in the back of the wagon, without thinking about anything, Rosario drove. Federico Farías was being escorted by a silent band of revolucionarios, dragging along without sorrow, ignorant of his plans and his politics. These men had no ideals or goals. They wore machetes slung across their backs, guns in their belts, and rifles over their shoulders. They followed a leader capable only of leading himself to hell, if he cared to go that far. And now they were following Federico Farías.

At the church, an elderly couple was trying to take their son's body home for proper mourning, but were impeded by several of Cobelo's men.

"The general said they'll be put in coffins right here, so that's how it will be."

The woman began pleading with the men, but her husband, knowing the futility of her efforts and fearful of the possible consequences, took her in his arms to calm her. The couple, and others like them, knelt in the rain by their dead family members. The cobelistas moved away, allowing them to mourn in peace.

The priest had already begun blessing the bodies and was sprinkling holy water when Rosario Alomar arrived.

Julián Vela and Jerónimo Pastor took the body of Federico Farías from the wagon and followed her. They placed the wrapped corpse on the ground, last in line.

The priest blessed the bodies, the families repeating with him, *Requiem aeterna donae dominus. Lux perpetua lucia deis.*

There were only six coffins in the whole town. No one had anticipated needing more. Doña Severina suddenly realized there was no coffin for Federico or for most of the others. The families had no idea what they were going to do.

Rosario spoke with Julián Vela. "Please tell your general that we don't have enough coffins. We need your help. We will pay you. And we would like to move the bodies into the church."

Not daring to look at her, Julián listened. Then, without a word, he walked away to find Serafín Machuca.

Valentín smiled as he chewed his cigar. "Get some men to help them make boxes." He blew a thick cloud of smoke. "And tell them they can move into the church. Come tell me when they're finished."

"Whatever you say, boss."

"One more thing. Tell the relatives they have to pay two pesos for each box. Except for the woman. I'll take care of hers."

"Sí, my general. When do you want them to hold the burials?"

"Tomorrow, after dawn. All at the same time. Don't be too rough on them, but make them follow your orders."

"Who, our men or the dead ones?" It was Serafín's way of letting Valentín know that his men would not be happy with the assignment.

Valentín smiled, understanding what Serafín meant.

"The families, Serafín. Don't be too hard on them. Our men should be happy with their pay. You bring me anyone who complains."

The men performed the unsavory chore without further incident—except that one oafish family member managed to shoot himself in the shoulder while using the butt of his pistol to hammer nails in a coffin.

Late that evening, Cipriano approached Valentín to see whether there were any new orders.

"Half the town is in that church."

"Good. Let them grieve. I want everyone at the burial tomorrow; I don't want a single person missing. Tell them I said so. Go on, then come back for dinner. I want to talk."

"Sure, muchacho. I kind of like this little show you've got going."

They laughed. Cipriano rode off on his horse. Valentín sat there in the shadow of the oil lamps, watching him disappear into the darkness.

Judging by scars and memories, he estimated that Cipriano must have been about forty when he had first known him. Valentín, age ten, had been ordered by his father to learn to ride a horse. Don Valentín Cobelo had declared that a man who can't ride is not a real man, not even trying to hide his disappointment at having had three daughters and only one son, and that child the youngest.

So Cipriano taught him to ride, without ever losing his patience or displaying any hint of anger—not because Valentín was the *patrón*'s son but because it was Cipriano's nature. He taught Valentín to love horses, to wash their sweaty bodies, to make them obey him out of loyalty rather than fear. He taught him to kill them when they broke a leg or became terminally ill.

In his loneliness, Valentín developed a deep affection for the ranch hand. Cipriano had no children of his own, at least not that he knew of. No woman had ever presented him with any. The boy was smart and courageous, but also stubborn and rebellious, traits that don Valentín mistook for cowardice. Wide-eyed, he was constantly searching for something new to look at. He would stare at an object until he knew everything there was to know about it. And he never uttered a sound when he fell off a horse, but instead proudly climbed back on, angry only with himself. The boy firmly believed Cipriano's words: "The horses aren't throwing you, muchacho, you're just not holding on tight enough. Remember that. It's true about more than just horses."

Being with Cipriano became a necessity for Valentín. The need grew stronger on those occasions when his father would tie him up for hours, sometimes all night long, in a corral with the livestock as punishment. He was punished for daring to cry, for not learning the differences between cows and bulls, mares and stallions, for refusing to brand them. With his arms and legs tied to the fencepost, numbed by excruciating pain, he would clench his teeth and cringe in terror at the phantoms that appeared in the shadows, wishing with all his soul that his father would die. He cried from fear and impotence, always with a fervent desire to escape, to break away into the desert with Cipriano and never return.

"Doesn't it feel like you're between two infinite spaces?" Cipriano had asked, his back flat on the earth, looking up at the dark sky, the first night he spent with the boy in that vast no-man's-land. "Look up at the stars and feel the earth," he told Valentín. "Grab it in your hands and feel it running through your fingers. It's like you are touching the stars. You can never be locked up, because all this is yours. Out here there is no time. Good and bad don't exist here, because nobody knows what's inside you, what you think or feel. And nobody can ever take that away from you, nobody. The sky's not afraid of anything, and the land never asks for explanations. They've learned to take whatever comes. These two infinite worlds must look at each other and swap stories like you and me. But they are strong and they will swallow the weak, you'll see. They know your fears better than you do. They'll tease and trick you, but if you can conquer them, you'll earn their respect and they'll let you be.

"They say all this used to be covered by ocean. How strong this land must be to have made the ocean go somewhere else, making waves in its hurry to get away! I've never seen the ocean, but I hear it still has waves. When did it recover from the shock of tangling with the desert? Must have been a long time ago. Just look out there, it's like nothing ever happened."

As dawn came, Cipriano told Valentín to run toward the sun.

He ran until he was completely out of breath, then threw himself on the still-cool sand, closing his eyes and feeling the sun on his body.

"See, muchacho, you can't touch it, but it's always there for you. Just keep your head up, let it cast a shadow on you. I've had to bow down too many times in my life."

"Do you ever feel hate, Cipriano?"

"Yes."

"Who do you hate?"

"That's my business."

"Tell me. I feel hate too. Is that bad? Mother says it is."

"Feeling hate isn't good or bad. It's just a way you feel."

"How do you start feeling hate?"

"There are lots of ways, too many to count."

"Tell me who you hate, Cipriano. You know I don't love my father. I think I hate him."

"Let's get going, boy, the horses must be thirsty."

In the desert with Cipriano, Valentín cried and mourned his mother's death the day she was buried. At the cemetery his father had warned him sternly. "Men don't cry about anything. Pull yourself together. Look at your sisters, they cry enough for everybody. If you want another mother, tell me and I'll take care of it."

"If you keep crying, boy, the pain will go away. Better keep it inside, then it will turn into strength deep inside you."

"Do you love Fidelia?"

"Yes, I love her."

"Is she your wife?"

"No, she's my woman. I had another one before, but I love Fidelia now."

"So why isn't Gudelia your daughter?"

"You ask too many questions."

"Come on, tell me. I want to understand."

"Because she had her with somebody else."

"Was she your woman then?"

"No. Everybody's got a past. The only comfort you can have in this lifetime is a woman. When she dies or leaves, you look for another one so you can stand it, just to make it through the night. If you don't have anybody to understand you, it wears on you. Without somebody whose eyes believe in you, who really knows you, life is hard to bear, muchacho. You can't live without loving somebody."

"I like Gudelia. Is that love?"

"That's how it starts."

"Do you think I could marry her?"

"The cook's daughter?" He laughed. "You're the patrón, boy. You haven't even seen a woman yet. Wait till you get older. How old are you?"

"Twelve. Are you going to teach me about women?"

"Women will teach you about women. You just have to let it happen. That's how you'll learn."

"I like Gudelia."

"She's pretty, but you'll see. She's not for you."

One night Valentín was doubled up with a pain he had never felt before and found himself in a terrible rage. When he arrived home he had seen Gudelia, naked, kneeling at Don Valentín's feet with his hands holding her head between his legs. Through his own tears, Valentín witnessed Gudelia's tears falling silently, in submission and humiliation, like drops of rain carried away by the wind.

Now a man of the desert, he had forgotten all about love until this afternoon, when those two crazed mares suddenly appeared in front of him. When would he experience Rosario Alomar's closeness again? He sat and waited patiently, looking out at the steady rain.

Santa María del Refugio had never been so brightly lit, not even on its saint's day. The coffins were made of rough, splintered wood and twisted nails only half hammered in; they completely filled the church. There were no crucifixes, except for a few that had been painted on.

The statue of the Virgin, gazing off in infinite wonder, refused to look down upon the scene at the base of her own pedestal. Grieving relatives were crushed up against the altar, along the aisles, around the coffins.

The prayers had become a deafening murmur, like the buzzing of bees after their honeycomb has been destroyed. The mourners' pleas rose to heaven amid the smell of wax, dried sweat, cold blood, and drying flowers, the pestilence of purgatory.

The priest called for a communal prayer to begin the rosary. It was Thursday. He paused for a moment, the irony of the situation weighing heavily; then he began the Joyous Mysteries.

"The First Mystery, the Annunciation to Mary. Our Father who art in heaven. . . ."

Only then did some of the cobelistas standing by the door take off their hats, cross themselves, and bow their heads, their machetes still slung across their backs.

Rosario Alomar couldn't concentrate on the prayers. Her thoughts and emotions wandered aimlessly as she sat next to her husband's body. She searched her memory for hazy images of her life with Federico, now abruptly ended, without good-byes or even an argument.

At her side, doña Severina sought comfort in the Virgin's face, the rosary beads moving mechanically between her nimble fingers. She had prayed with this same rosary for her husband's return from Cuba, but he never came. Half thinking she could hide the truth from God, later she had prayed that he be dead and not living with some woman, especially not a black or mulatto woman. She had also used it to pray for the strength to raise her daughter and for God to protect them both. She used it to pray for a good husband for Rosario. And now she pleaded for the eternal rest of her son-in-law's soul and for God, in His infinite goodness, once again to show mercy on her and her daughter.

"Glory to the Father, to the Son, and to the Holy Spirit. Amen. The Third Mystery, the birth of the Son of God. . . ."

In those moments of prayer and solitude, Rosario Alomar's thoughts formed a picture of Valentín Cobelo galloping toward her on his horse. She did not quite remember his face, just a figure suddenly appearing and circling around her carriage. She looked at Federico's coffin and cried without making a sound, her sorrow gone limp.

36

Then she remembered the rain. It must be an omen. She got up and made her way to the vestibule, where she uncovered her head and let the rain pour down her face. It was a soothing balm for her body. She stood there with her eyes closed. The rain was for her alone; she opened herself to it, arms spread, holding nothing back. Her wet hands caressed her body, the rain following the path she had traced for it, the rivulets becoming a river.

"They're still praying in the church, Valentín, even some of our men." Cipriano was sitting next to the general.

"There are some things those men will never get rid of."

"You just don't understand them, General. Got a cigarette?"

"I want her, Cipriano." Without looking at him, Valentín gave him a cigar and some matches.

"Then take her. It wouldn't be the first time. And, God willing, it won't be the last."

Valentín looked at him. Cipriano was concentrating on the preparation of his cigar, wetting it with his tongue. He knew that Valentín wanted to see his eyes.

"She'll come without my having to take her."

"If that's how you want it, that's how it'll be."

"That woman—I don't know if it's love. I don't know if I could love her. But I want to have her near; she's a part of me."

"Then have her near; if not, you'll never get her off your mind."

"The rain is almost finished. Tomorrow we'll see the sun again, Cipriano. Tomorrow we'll see each other again."

"It's only the beginning, Valentín."

Serafín Machuca and Cipriano were eating supper with Valentín in the municipal building, by the light of oil lamps. The rain ran down the windowpanes outside this room, which had been the mayor's office before he died the previous day. Flames flickered around them, enclosing them in a hole in the night.

Only Valentín used a knife and fork, borrowed from a near-by home, to eat. The others ate their food with bread and tortillas. He sipped red wine. They washed their food down with warm beer.

"They're quiet, General, but restless." Serafín spoke without taking his eyes off his plate.

"Our people?"

"Yeah. Even with the two pesos, they don't like this setup."

"They don't know what's going on and it makes them nervous," Cipriano added.

"Yeah, that's it. They haven't said anything, General, but they're getting real edgy. It was okay at first, the chase and the fight and all, but then suddenly you told us to stop, for no reason. No women, no loot, nothing; just stop. Then they had to make those boxes for the bodies. That's what did it, the boxes. They're restless, like lost wolves, but they're not howling, and that's what worries me," Serafín spoke hurriedly as he ate, scooping up his food with a tortilla.

"I just need a little more time here, Serafín. I'll find them a reward."

"Look, General, I understand you. You know you can count on me. But this bunch of fools doesn't think. They don't know you like I do. When their blood boils, they've gotta do something about it. That's just how they are, and we want them that way."

"No whorehouses around here, either," muttered Cipriano.

Valentín smiled. He poured more wine for himself and offered some to Cipriano.

"Send them a message. Let them know you understand them, that you're thinking about them. Ask them to help you by waiting." Cipriano sipped his wine. "I still can't get used to this stuff. It doesn't taste strong enough. I started drinking it too late; my throat's already ruined."

"They'll get over it. Tell them I feel the same way they do. Things'll get better soon. Tell them I appreciate their help with the coffins. You still haven't told me how many we lost."

"Not many, General. Dead, only six. About ten wounded, but they're still wandering around. It's the locals who died. Between them and the federales, they really got hit hard. Then we got here and it was all over." Serafín smiled.

"I want the people in the village to think they were killed by their own men and the federales. Keep it all between them," warned Valentín.

Serafín was rolling the words around in his mouth before he dared to speak them out loud. "Let's just take the whole damn town, General."

Valentín did not answer, but his face registered irritation.

"Forgive me, General. You know better than I do, especially when it's your business. I'm just an idiot. I better get going and deliver your message." He jumped up, grabbed his hat, and, as he reached the door, was relieved to hear Valentín's voice.

"Just stay calm."

Serafín bowed his head and left the room.

"It makes them nervous that they haven't seen you."

"They'll see me tomorrow. Everyone will see me tomorrow, Cipriano."

"Where are you going to sleep, muchacho?"

"Upstairs. Rarámuri made me a bed. You sleep down here."

Hurried footsteps sounded outside. There was a loud knock at the door. It was Julián Vela. Cipriano let him in.

"What brings you here, Julián?" Valentín poured himself more wine.

"I don't want to get involved in other people's business, General, but I thought you should know what I saw." Valentín waited quietly for him to proceed. "A gentleman— you know, like you—came to the house looking for doña Rosario, the widow, and he's there with her now, her and the mother. He's well dressed, looks rich. I thought you'd want to know." Julián glanced longingly at the bottle of wine.

Valentín sat quietly for a moment. Julián sensed Cipriano's approval. He knew he had done the right thing and awaited his general's orders.

"You should be there now keeping an eye on them." Valentín winked at him.

"Sí, General. I was just leaving." He licked his lips and dared to ask. "Could I have a little sip of your wine?"

"Go ahead, pour yourself some."

Julián approached the table, poured himself half a glass, and drank it in two gulps.

"Thank you, General. I'll be leaving now. I must get back." He left with a bounce in his step, closing the door with great care.

"Cipriano, tomorrow, before they go to the burial, make sure you know who he is and where he lives."

"Do you want me to report back to you?"

Valentín Cobelo nodded, stood up, and took one of the lamps. Cipriano started up the stairs with Valentín following him. Their steps sounded hollow on the wooden treads. Their shadows climbed with them, gliding along the ceiling. There was no other sound. They felt the rain but could not hear it. Valentín lay down on his bed. Cipriano sat in a corner and waited for Valentín to fall asleep. Once he was asleep, Cipriano lowered the lamp and went downstairs. He was tired. Before surrendering to sleep on one of the couches, he thought about Rosario Alomar. He had never seen her, but he didn't need to. Passions can be smelled, like rainstorms. They warn you of their fury, but you can't stop them.

FOUR

DAWN CREPT INTO MONREAL THROUGH THE OPEN DOOR OF the church of Santa María del Refugio. The mourning families, huddled around their dead, awakened slowly. The seemingly endless night, the vigil, and sheer exhaustion had drained them of most of their tears. The votives and pillar candles, lit at the wake, were now nearly consumed, as if they had surrendered to the intensity of emotion. A few, lit in the late hours of sleeplessness, still twinkled brightly.

Rosario Alomar had slept only sporadically. Efraín Gutiérrez was beside her, his bolo tie still tight around his shirt collar and his mother and sister nearby, as if to camouflage his intentions. The neighbors, in their pain, glanced at them furtively through swollen eyes. Doña Severina slept quietly, her rosary, abandoned in the middle of one of the Holy Mysteries, still dangling from her fingers.

In the vestibule several cobelistas slept sitting against the walls, shrouded against the cold desert night. Others busied themselves outside, lighting fires and preparing breakfast in the deserted streets. Somewhere a faint melody danced in the air: *Loneliness is my only companion; I long for your return.*

Uncertainly, slowly, the sun appeared, fresh and free of all memory and nostalgia. The rain, tired and wrung out, had gone somewhere else.

The church bells rang at five-thirty as they did every morning, waking up those few still asleep. Today they also served to announce the burials. The priest began organizing the procession to the cemetery. Mourners and keepers alike stirred. Those fortunate not to have to face a loved one's bed, made and forevermore untouched, lit lamps that shone timidly through the windows. Then, in small groups, they made their way to the church to join the procession and to help carry the coffins.

Walking slowly in their grief, the townspeople barely noticed the twenty cobelistas on horseback, galloping in the opposite direction. The clatter of hoofbeats on the cobblestones marked their passing, their horses dancing around the potholes left behind by the rain. No one turned to watch as they passed out of town out into the desert.

Cipriano climbed up to where Valentín had slept. He was awake now, with his hands interlaced behind his head and his eyes fixed on the ceiling.

"She's inside me, Cipriano, in here," he said, indicating his chest.

"Yeah, she's got you all right, muchacho. That's how it was

with me too, with my Fidelia, days and nights, not when I met her but when the fever took her. She was right here, but I couldn't hold her anymore."

"Another debt my father left behind."

"You just worry about yourself, muchacho. It won't last long enough, even if it lasts till you die."

The first long box emerged from the doorway of Santa María del Refugio carried by four men. The cobelistas were standing nearby, hats firmly planted on their heads, machetes and rifles in their hands.

Valentín approached Cipriano and sat down next to him.

"Did you do what I asked?"

"I sent Serafín. I told him to take some of the restless ones. Jerónimo Pastor went too. Julián and Rarámuri are on the lookout around here, keeping the others in line."

The coffins were lined up one after another all the way to the holy ground on the outskirts of Monreal. The wailing had resumed and sobs spread through the contingent like a fire fanned by winds blowing over open fields. Even this early it was already hot.

Serafín Machuca and the others rode slowly, trotting across the dry countryside, making their way through cactus and yucca.

The procession of mourners reached Margaritas Street. Rosario Alomar walked arm in arm with her mother. Efraín Gutiérrez walked next to her.

Valentín and Cipriano were eating beans and drinking their third cup of coffee.

Draped in black and gold, the priest led the way. Next

44

came the sacristan, rhythmically swinging the smoking incense burner on its heavy chain. He was followed by two acolytes holding gold crosses high in the air. They had forgotten the bell.

Valentín lit a cigarette and offered one to Cipriano.

The earth had sucked up the puddles; only a few shoes, boots, and sandals actually got wet.

Serafín Machuca spied the Gutiérrez ranch, La Giralda, and headed toward it without quickening his pace.

The pallbearers, in their black suits and bolo ties, could feel the sweat running down their temples, foreheads, and necks. Efraín Gutiérrez offered to replace one of the men carrying the coffin of Federico Farías. From a distance the cobelistas watched the procession, which was joined here and there by more townspeople. The children walked along in silence, occasionally daring to look up and stare at the strangers, then getting their ears boxed for being so impertinent.

On Serafín Machuca's order his men rushed toward the main house, dropping their reins, their machetes held high and rifles spitting bullets.

Valentín Cobelo rose from his chair when he saw her approach, walking tall and bearing her weariness proudly, like an expensive piece of jewelry. Valentín felt her presence in his stomach and in his groin. He allowed his desire to roam free and encompass her.

Three or four ranch hands quickly overcame their shock and started shooting back. Others tried to flee, but death hit them in the back, the chest, the face. The women from the kitchen and some of the cleaning women were drawn out by the noise. When they realized what was happening, they ran wherever their fear carried them.

Rosario Alomar recognized Valentín Cobelo. She looked at him as he stared at her. There was no denying his presence and the effect he had on her. His face, which she had been unable to remember earlier that morning, seemed to emerge from deep within her, bursting from her chest, tearing open her intestines, seeping over her skin. She felt faint and clutched her mother's arm tighter. She closed her eyes and summoned all her remaining strength just to keep walking.

Using the powerful hooves of their crazed horses to kick in the doors, Serafín Machuca and Jerónimo Pastor entered the house, furiously spurring their horses, destroying everything in sight. The rest of the men followed, opening every cabinet and drawer, rummaging, grabbing, and carrying off all they could drag with them. The cobelistas' cries of glee were as loud as the havoc they wreaked. Efraín Gutiérrez's mother and sister, frozen in terror, clung frantically to each other at the top of the stairs. Jerónimo Pastor galloped straight toward them. "No!" yelled Serafín Machuca, and Jerónimo turned his horse at the last instant to avoid trampling the women. Serafín and the others mounted the stairs, entering the bed-rooms, machetes in hand.

Valentín stared at Rosario's back until she was swallowed up by the procession. She didn't dare turn her head, yet she could still see that face, branded in her soul. She tried to purge it, but she couldn't. She only managed to close her eyes as the men began to dig graves for Federico and the others.

The cobelistas burned all the buildings at La Giralda. They torched curtains, furniture, blankets, sheets.

Valentín Cobelo had returned to his chair, his anxiety tucked back into place.

They killed or scared off the cattle and made their way back into the house, where they found the servant women hiding and, quickly dismounting, ripped their blouses off and had their way with them, rewarding the women and girls for their service by not killing them. Only one resisted and lost a breast to an angry machete. Efraín's mother and sister felt the world caving in under the heat of the flames.

The men of Monreal were still digging graves. When they were deep enough, they began lowering the coffins into the ground. Praying in Latin, the priest commended the dead to God for all eternity while the mourners threw handfuls of dirt on the coffins. Only then was Rosario Alomar able to tear herself away from thoughts of Valentín Cobelo and say good-bye to Federico Farías. She didn't speak, but rather watched, as his coffin was slowly covered with red and yellow dirt flecked with small stones. Efraín Gutiérrez crossed himself and stood quietly with his hands behind his back, waiting.

Breaking into a full gallop, Serafín Machuca and his men raced away from La Giralda, leaving it completely engulfed in flames.

Valentín went inside. He didn't want to wait for Rosario
Alomar to return.

The townspeople, with the hot sun pressing tight against
their bodies, wandered slowly back to Monreal. The last of
the puddles had long since been completely devoured by the
earth. Some faces were tearstained, others were simply sad,
but all were grief-stricken.

Silently, Efraín Gutiérrez took Rosario Alomar's arm and
walked beside her. Rosario was still holding her mother's arm.
Somehow, without realizing it, they had turned down a different street and bypassed the municipal building altogether.

The cobelistas quietly watched the mourners pass. There
were no sounds of laughter or loud voices. The cooking fires
had been extinguished.

Upon arriving at Rosario's house, Efraín Gutiérrez said
good-bye at the door. "Doña Rosario, doña Severina, I am at
your service. Please call on me for anything that you might
need."

"Really, don Efraín, you have no idea how grateful we are
for your kindnesses. As you can see, my daughter and I are
quite alone again."

"Don't worry, señora. All this will soon be behind us."

"Thank you, don Efraín," was all Rosario said.

"I will call on you again tomorrow. Try to get some rest. I
hope by then they'll all be gone and our lives can get back to
normal." Efraín put on his hat and walked away.

Monreal was lifeless the rest of the day. There were no
dreams save those of exhaustion, no strength other than the
oppressive heat. The townspeople were already trying to erase
their memories, to turn this interminable present into an
undetectable scar. They locked themselves behind heavy

doors and shuttered windows, hoping to take refuge there, never again to face the world that had butchered their simple lives. They believed they had been truly happy before all this had happened. Before, sorrow had been a quaint story or polite parlor conversation. And they had told the same stories over and over again.

The cobelistas had been appeased. Those who went with Serafín Machuca told the others of their adventure and, laughing, bragged of naked flesh and showed off their stolen treasures, some of which they shared: silverware, chains, medallions, rings, silver spurs. They all laughed, trying to endure the endless waiting.

Later that afternoon, Valentín Cobelo appeared at Rosario Alomar's house. Cipriano, Serafín Machuca, and Rarámuri waited on their horses nearby.

Valentín knocked without removing his hat. Doña Severina opened the door. She didn't know what to say to this man, but she knew, looking at him for the first time, that he was already part of Rosario's life—and of hers.

He courteously removed his hat. "Good afternoon, señora. I am Valentín Cobelo."

Severina had to stifle a sudden urge to cross herself. She looked back inside the house for Rosario, fearing for her without knowing why.

Rosario came to the door and shivered with surprise when she realized the moment she had been waiting and wishing for had come. She was finally facing him. The silence and her tangled nerves were shattered by a desperate scream.

"Valentín Cobelo! You are a murderer! I have come to kill you!"

Efraín Gutiérrez stood there, his clothes filthy and soaked

through with sweat, his eyes moist with tears. He held a pistol in his shaky hand, barely containing his pain and rage.

Rarámuri and Serafín Machuca approached him menacingly, but Cipriano motioned for them to stop.

Rosario and her mother closed the door partway, momentarily blocking Valentín Cobelo from view.

"Murderer! Come out, you bastard!" Efraín yelled, his scratchy voice barely audible.

Valentín stepped away from the women and approached Efraín. Neighbors looked out their windows, this new shock rousing them from their grief.

"Who have I killed? I haven't even left town. I have witnesses." Valentín spoke calmly without raising his voice. He was sizing up Efraín's gestures, his size, his courage.

"Liar! You killed my men; you burned my house. I'm going to kill you!"

Rarámuri stood there with a machete in his hand.

"A man who is going to kill someone doesn't announce it, he just does it," murmured Cipriano. "This man doesn't have the courage."

"These are hard times. We're in the middle of a revolution. You're still alive, you still have your mother and sister. Go get them and leave town." Valentín walked over to Efraín and knocked the gun out of his hand. Then he bent down and, after unloading it, threw it a distance away. Shamed and in shock, Efraín dropped to the ground, felled by his own impotence. Valentín turned his back and walked toward Rosario Alomar, who had been approaching Efraín.

"Come, get up, you must go," she said, with compassion in her voice. "It's not worth the humiliation."

He got up without raising his head, beaten, his manhood crushed, and disappeared down the first dirt road that offered to hide him. He didn't even mount his horse. That would have required a strength he no longer possessed.

The shadows cast by Rosario and Valentín's bodies stretched out over the cobblestones. As she turned toward him, she could not think. She could only feel want, desire. Valentín drew closer. Rosario Alomar clenched her teeth tightly and slapped his face once, twice; as she prepared for her third strike, he caught her hand in midair, linking their bodies. Their breaths and desires mingled. Valentín grabbed her and kissed her, conquering the hidden urges beating behind those reticent lips. She was unwilling to give away with just a kiss the life that had already been snatched from her by his desperate mouth, but he did not give up and finally triumphed. Rosario knew she belonged to this man, knew his manhood was meant for her, was hers. She pressed herself into his broad chest as if leaping from a precipice into another world. He pulled away, holding her more with his eyes than with his arms, and whispered into her ear.

"Everything, Rosario, everything!"

Rosario reached to caress his cheek but, before she even touched him, a fearful premonition brought her back to reality, rekindling her desire to get away from him, to be free. It tore her soul, ripped her away from his eyes, screamed within her. "Everything" was too much! "Everything" was more than the sky and the desert and the rain and her dreams. She ran into the house, leaving the door open behind her, allowing Valentín Cobelo's eyes to follow her. Brimming with something close to enchantment, he mounted his horse and galloped off yelling, with his men in close pursuit, all of them wrapped in dust they stole from the wounded earth.

FIVE

ROSARIO'S HEART WAS ENTANGLED LIKE A TREE TRUNK ON A riverbank, starving for love yet afraid of its passion, caught by surprise.

Once again she was engulfed in loneliness, though she had banished it five years ago. The years she had spent married to Federico Farías were already turning into dust, like his body would. Is life nothing more than memories? The mere idea brought tears to her eyes, and she was a woman who never cried. Safe in the bedroom that had harbored her as a child, a young woman, and finally a barren wife, whose dreams of a family of her own were shattered by a series of crushing miscarriages, she found a few tears were good company. She had cried on the lap of her papá, her loving father, who had gone away one day, telling her, "Take care of your mother. I'll be back, Rosario. Something far away is calling me. I can't explain what I feel, why I'm going. Something is crumbling, but you must be strong, my darling." And he left. The rest of her adolescence was spent in a haze of sadness. The best way to endure it, she learned, was to harden her soul, protect herself from herself and from all others. She learned to smile at unhappiness. By the time she realized this she was already a woman with many memories. In the words of doña Nicasia Maytorena, her mother's friend, men either die or they leave you. Then loneliness strikes and makes the absence even more painful.

The sun was lazy. Its rays fell like tired eyelids on the face of the sleepy afternoon. Who is he? A stranger, like so many other things in life that I let pass by while I took care of Mamá to protect myself, always restrained. Where is he? Everything seemed far away. Sleep took her, forced her across an expanse of time, and deposited her in her bed.

I didn't love Federico, even Mamá knew it, but it was good to have him at my side with his tenderness, his innocence, his childlike caresses, his youthful exuberance in my body, his face nestled against me. What is love? A big question to ask at thirty. There is no answer. Only a meeting, an encounter.

Now I must lock up my body, my womb, my thighs, my breasts. Hide them day and night, only let them escape in lonely, desolate caresses, secret and unsatisfying. Steal my own desire and hide it from myself. Use my body only to move around, to be, to sleep and awaken, to pass time. No more desperation, no more surrendering to that unmentionable need. Only correctness, punishment. Never look at men again, I'm beyond that now. My lips. Here, here, again. Why?

Where is he? Who is he? That strength, that chest, that courage, that sure calm voice, that ability to overwhelm. That man can't feel love. But I can, and I won't love him. His kiss still haunts me, traps me. I know he's not gone. He's flowing in my blood, running through my body, ever since I felt his closeness: such a hard, barren land, a vastness I can already feel. Bite my lips. Don't let him get away. His hands on my arms, in my hair. He absorbs me with his gaze, drowns me. I can't hide from him. Even before, on the day of the massacre, when I went looking for Federico and first saw him, I came back with a crater in my chest where the winds of passion were already blowing. How much longer can I hold them back?

Tears run through me like water surging from a spring. A blinding brilliance. Why think? Thinking only causes suffering. It's amazing how I can create tasks to hide behind, nimbly moving the knitting needles without piercing my heart or even a finger, so as not to remind myself of the blood flowing inside. What am I thinking about? This is no time to laugh.

What must Mamá think about all this? Always looking up to heaven, praying for hope. What would she do if I told her I'm going away with that man and I can't take her with me, it's just one of those sudden, unexpected things in life? Pity keeps me with you, Mamá, but now I don't know whether the pity I feel is for you or for me.

Cry. One doesn't cry for others, only for oneself. Is that wrong, to cry for myself? I want to run out screaming, to flee, to escape and never find myself again. I don't want to be me anymore. I am a woman, but it is so hard to really feel like a woman, to know myself as a woman.

Keep crying, don't hold back. Women always cry, everyone says so. We don't even need a reason; we are women. Crying is what women do. Part of being a woman is having that freedom.

"Why are you crying, Rosario?" asked Severina, not really expecting an answer, but rather to comfort her daughter with tenderness. "It seems like only yesterday that your doll broke. Then you stained your new dress with bread pudding. I can still remember when you cried, afraid of not being a little girl any longer. Ay, Dios mío, my God, you have grown into such a woman."

Her face buried in a pillow, Rosario kept on crying, holding nothing back. Severina sat beside her, gently lifted Rosario's head, and placed it on her lap. She knew this was not a time for her to cry too, so she channeled her own tears into soft caresses, tenderly stroking Rosario's hair and face.

"Cry, hija, cry all you can. Just let go. When the crying stops, in that first moment of silence you'll know the answer. You've known all along, you just don't want to admit it."

"I'm afraid, Mamá."

"Fear is nothing to worry about, but you must watch out for bitterness."

"I'm too weak, Mamá." Rosario put her arm around her mother's waist and drew herself nearer.

"No, hija, you are too strong." Severina struggled to hold back tears.

"Well, then, I no longer have the strength to keep on being strong. I'm so tired. When will night come, so I can rest? I just want to sleep. When will it all go away?"

"It will pass soon enough. Then other things will come. Don't be afraid, Rosario, you will always be strong, you'll see."

"I don't know what I feel. It's overwhelming."

"Look at your tears. They are not the tears of fear." And Severina smiled, and was silent. She didn't want to destroy the serenity of the moment.

They remained bound to each other, light pouring in through the window and raining down on their backs.

Rosario's tears subsided, dripping now like leaks of fragile thought. Her mother's body was a refuge. She held tighter to prolong the sense of peace and comfort it gave her. She sought an anchorage to keep the river flowing inside her from rushing her toward an unknown sea, like the river that had swept away her father. It had been a long time since she had lost herself so completely in her mother's love. She felt a strong need to love her mother again, a need that had faded with the monotony of daily routine. Perhaps their clinging was born of a mutual eagerness to deny the possibility that one would ever abandon the other, leaving both alone.

Rosario's closeness filled Severina with the warm glow of motherhood. It was rhythmic, like the waves of the ocean, crashing, then retreating. She had shelved these tender feelings as her daughter grew up and became a strong woman. But now her daughter's strength wavered in the face of this overpowering passion that had thrust itself into their lives. She had understood everything when she opened the door to that man. Her soul, forged by daily defeat, told her she had wasted her life waiting for her husband to return. Looking back, she couldn't even find comfort in the knowledge that she had at least tried to avoid becoming a victim of old age, alone with her memories.

I am the one who is afraid, Rosario, afraid that you will do what I could never do. I never thought of another man, never dared to: I was already old when Celestino left, nearly forty when I had you. But you, hija, I know you will do it, even if you don't know it yet. How could I not understand when I have seen you, felt you, lived your life every day? I didn't even risk being a woman for myself, Rosario. Can you understand that? How could you? You are so strong and sure of yourself. When did I lose

my destiny? Sometimes I think I never really had one. Dios mío.
Your father was no destiny. He was just a husband who left.
When I met Celestino he was no more than a good man with a
little money who had come from Cuba. Why did he even bother
coming here if he was just going to turn around and go back?
He told us so many stories. I can still see him drawing birds and
flowers for you and describing the sugar harvest celebrations.
Before I realized it, he was gone. You'll leave me too; there's
nothing I can do to prevent it. I don't want you to give up your
life for me, you've done enough. But, oh, to have felt passion, just
once! I've only seen it pass by. Ay, Dios mío, take care of this
child, watch over her for me.

Severina kissed Rosario, her lips lingering to prolong the
contact. Her daughter hugged her again tightly, letting a joyous murmur escape. She turned to look up at her mother's
face. There were no tears, but a soft sadness veiled her loving
eyes.

Without warning or mercy, the sound of the bells of Santa
María del Refugio hammered down upon them, announcing
the first of the nine rosaries in memory of Monreal's recent
dead.

"Can't we wait a bit longer, Mamá? I don't want to go out.
I don't want to see anyone."

"We have to go, hija. It's just one rosary." Severina gathered her daughter's hair in her hands.

More like an eternity. Constant repetition. More confusion
when I am already confused enough. I don't have any more
tears. Breathe. Air. Wind blowing through the streets, caressing
the windows. No time for a bath, just a quick wash-up, a change
of clothes to give the impression of a fresh appearance. No need
to try and achieve a particular facial expression, it would be a

lie anyway. Anyway, nobody will know what's brewing inside me, Rosario Alomar, widow of Federico Farías. They'll say I'm beautiful. But I am tired, jaded. I wish I could stay here inside, not see the world again until even trying to forget is forgotten. The brush finds its way through my hair, tugging, becoming part of the tangle. No dark circles under my eyes. What would he think if he saw me now? He won't, he won't ever see me again. We'll leave this place. No one will know where we've gone. My heart beats faster. I'm under his spell again. I can't lie to myself. I can see myself in the mirror, desires and all. He's there too, mirrored in my face.

The bells rang a second time.

"Hurry, hija. Put on this black dress. You must wear mourning clothes."

Black. Me in mourning? I have always despised death. I'd rather wear red or pink with yellow and orange ribbons, get past all this and keep running so it can't catch up with me. Splash warm water on my face. I'd love a hot, steaming bath, submerge myself, revel in my body, close my eyes and see him again.

"Let's go, Mamá."

As they crossed over the threshold they joined arms, but still seeped in melancholy. It was like the other time, when grieving for Celestino had passed and loneliness had become a way of life.

It was six o'clock in the evening, and mourning relatives, faithful families, and friends filled Santa María del Refugio. Rosario sensed that all those faces, bodies, silhouettes, and shadows knew that Valentín Cobelo had kissed her lips openly in the street, without pretense or respect. Back among the living, back on earth, her heart closed tightly and her body held erect, a smile worked its way from deep inside her, coming to full bloom on her lips.

To clear her mind, Rosario prayed. She gave in to the rhythmic cadence of the Hail Marys, the Lord's Prayer, the Glorias, the sermon. The Latin words seeped in and emptied her mind, isolated her, made her forget, gave her respite. Images of the wake threatened to invade her reverie, but she took refuge in the Ora Pro Nobis.

She would rather have run away from that place, from those tedious words of death and heaven and resurrection, tears and suffering in this lifetime and eternal glory in the life hereafter. Yet she remained still, her gazed lowered, and distracted herself by studying her hands. She didn't need to resurrect herself. The priest's final blessing was like a door opened wide, the fresh air a welcome gift on a clear summer evening.

As the parishioners emptied out of the church, Rosario noticed their barely concealed looks of disapproval, hidden behind greetings, mutual condolences, and hugs and kisses. She stunned them all with her scorn. They'll soon forget about it, she thought.

Doña Esther Fonseca and doña Nicasia Maytorena, family friends and frequent visitors to the Alomar home, had no relatives killed in the battle but they were fervent attendees at any rosary and offered to come for a short visit, "Now that we all four are widows."

The older women had their hair piled high on top of their heads, fluffed up with pride and piety, and wore pleated silk muslin, velvet and taffeta capes, and simple black veils over their faces; Rosario's hair was loosely gathered with an embroidered ribbon from Brussels and cascaded over her shoulders under a long black mantilla. They strolled in pairs, arm in arm.

Rosario walked with doña Nicasia Maytorena, who had known her since Rosario and her own daughter, Martha, were little girls. She and Severina used to make plans for their daughters, back when their husbands, so gallant and handsome, still danced La Graciana with them and played *puncho* and *tute*. Celestino had brought men and women together—at separate tables, of course—to play these new games. Doña Esther walked slightly ahead with Severina and reminisced about her Leonicio. Severina was an accomplished listener, and her quiet willingness to hear the same tired memories made Esther feel understood and appreciated. The ladies' skirts brushed the ground, and gradually dust crept up their hems. The rustling of their dresses made it impossible to hear their footsteps, since they all wore soft flat-heeled boots.

The Alomar living room was impeccably furnished in wood and brocade, softly lit by oil lamps. Having already said it as she left the church, doña Esther repeated herself: "Father Ignacio's sermon was just lovely. He really seems to care about us, even though he is from San Luis."

"How long has he been here now?" asked Severina, as Rosario served the lemonade. "About ten years, isn't it?"

"No, longer than that. He was the one who buried my husband, may he rest in peace, and that was eleven years ago this April," corrected doña Esther.

"I'll go make some hot chocolate," offered Rosario, trying to keep the conversation from bringing up any dates that would be painful for her mother.

The three women waited in silence for Rosario to leave the room. "Federico certainly picked a fine time to become a national hero." Doña Esther shook her head in disbelief.

"Oh, don't say that. If my husband were still alive, I'm sure he would have done the same thing."

"Yes, Nicasia, and you would still be a widow, crying like Mary Magdalene."

"I've never been one to cry much. Of course, I cried when he died, but that's normal. A woman's husband only dies once."

"Federico was an idealist, that's all," said Severina, eyeing doña Esther.

"The only thing gained by all that idealism is the suffering and misery of this whole town. That and the fact that your daughter is a widow at the age of thirty." Doña Esther fluffed the ruffles at her wrists.

"They came looking for Federico," doña Severina clarified. "He didn't go out on the street recruiting martyrs."

"Here comes Rosario," whispered doña Nicasia. "We were saying, Rosario, that we all cared very much for Federico. He was very respected. There is no doubt he would have gone far. Isn't that right, Esther?" And doña Nicasia looked right at her friend.

"Oh, yes, and such goodness in his heart. No one ever saw him get angry."

"Yes, that's true," agreed Rosario. "He rarely got upset."

"I still don't quite understand how it all happened," doña Esther went on. "They say the revolucionarios shot only at the federales, but—"

Doña Nicasia kicked doña Esther lightly.

"Rosario, if you'll bring the cups," said Severina, "I'll get the chocolate."

"Let me take care of it, Mamá," said Rosario. She stood and left the room.

"Really, Esther, how indelicate of you. All your talk about revolucionarios!"

"Hush, Rosario will hear you!" warned doña Esther.

Rosario returned, carrying a wooden tray with silver handles, laden with cups and a steaming pitcher of chocolate. "I just love hot chocolate," she said, as she began to serve the ladies. "Here, have some butter cookies. Mamá made them this morning. We are so glad you came."

"Thank you, darling. You know how much we love you."

"So tell me, what are they saying about the revolucionarios?" Rosario looked straight at doña Nicasia and doña Esther.

The ladies exchanged quick, nervous glances. Now they were forced to confront what they had been trying to avoid. They made silly remarks about the chocolate and how hot it was, and doña Nicasia tried to brush off the question. "Oh, not much, really. I think, more than anything else, it's been such a shock to everyone. It's usually so quiet around here."

"Yes, but what are they saying?" Rosario sat holding the cup and saucer in her hand, blowing softly on her chocolate. "You know what I mean."

She's the same as always, thought Severina.

Doña Nicasia looked at doña Esther, begging her with her eyes to speak first.

"Ah, niñita, it's just talk. They don't really say anything. There's nothing to say. All things considered, I'd say they've behaved rather well. We've all heard stories about revolucionarios. They *have* been talking about the leader, though. What's his name?" Doña Esther looked at doña Nicasia.

"Valentín Cobelo," Rosario answered, in a strong voice and without hesitation. It was the first time she had ever spoken his name.

The room closed in and held the name aloft. The visiting ladies were taken aback as much by the sound as by the manner in which it was spoken, almost like an invocation. Severina stared into her cup.

"An interesting man, no doubt. He doesn't look much like an Indio—the opposite, really." Doña Nicasia was still trying to calm her nerves.

"He's handsome, and he looks very young. Well, I haven't really seen him, but that's what they say. But I'm sure he must be a terrible man. I can imagine the anguish you must have suffered, Rosario." Doña Esther shot her a stern look.

"No, you can't," answered Rosario, without a trace of sarcasm in her voice.

"Everyone says it was you who got his men to help with the coffins, and you showed great courage when you slapped his face. But you never can tell what a man like that is capable of. Just look at what happened to poor Efraín Gutiérrez," doña Esther said.

"Has he left?" ventured Severina.

"In shame," said doña Esther.

"While we're on the subject, there are some people who say this man already knew you, and that he came here because—"

"That's ridiculous!" Rosario shot up from her chair, furious. "I've never seen him before in my life!"

"Hija, please. It's not Esther or Nicasia's fault."

"I know, I'm sorry. I'm not angry with them." Rosario paced, trying to contain the urge to break something. She turned to face them. "If he already knew me, why didn't he just take me away? Why didn't I leave with him? Silly gossips."

"Calm down, Rosario. It was just idle chatter, nothing more. I don't even know why you mentioned it, Nicasia."

"May God punish me if my daughter knew that man," said Severina, truly offended.

"Now tell me something, Rosario. Did you embrace that man? Did he really force himself on you?"

"Esther, that is none of our business."

"Thank you, doña Nicasia. What do you think, doña Esther?" Rosario challenged the older woman with her eyes.

"What did you expect? He would have killed my daughter if she had refused!"

"And if I really did choose to let him hug me and kiss me, what then? Does that give everyone in this town the right to judge me?"

"To hell with all this nonsense!" Doña Nicasia hated seeing the girl trapped. "I think that every once in a while we women should do what we want. What you have done is your business." She took a sip of her chocolate.

Rosario stood, walked toward her, and kissed her on the cheek.

"I only asked the question because of the consequences it may bring."

"And what consequences might those be, Esther?" asked Severina.

"Everyone—well, almost everyone, even those who don't think Rosario knew that man before—they're talking about what will happen when he comes back."

"Why are they worried about that?" Rosario was beginning to understand doña Esther's real apprehension.

"They're nervous. I don't know. I think they're afraid of what you might do and what that man could do." Doña Nicasia spoke as plainly as she was able.

Doña Esther looked at her with exasperation. "That man will return, don't you doubt it. You have to think about it very carefully, Rosario."

"You want to know what I'm going to do? I'll tell you, so

this town of gossips and meddlers knows for certain. I'm going to do whatever the hell I want!"

"*Rosario!*"

Rosario! Rosario! There was an incessant crying of her name in the recesses of Valentín Cobelo's soul. He rode blindly in the desert, wanting only to reach his hideout, a refuge between two lonely hills left behind by the retreating sea. The vastness faded with nightfall, only to become an endless horizon again in the sunlight. The desert watched over him, adopted him.

This desert will be yours too, Rosario, because all that I am will be yours. There will be no curve of your body that will escape the sand. You will wake during the night and hear the footsteps of the wind bringing you closer to my body, where you will bury yourself. I will plant you here like a seed. You and the sun will become one. Only I will know that its brilliance, its splendor, is you, Rosario. My Rosario.

The earth opened to the footsteps of the sweaty, tired horses. The desert was waiting for their return, this desert that only Valentín Cobelo's galloping men traveled, stamping and cracking open. They dragged the sun with them, immersing themselves in it. They were covered with the dust they had stirred up for the wind to swallow.

When desperation has conquered you, when you feel you can't go on any longer, when you are exploding because you don't know where or how to find me, when your fear of being mine becomes the fear of not being mine, I will come back for you, Rosario. Then it will be forever. And the earth will swallow us both.

SIX

THE WIND WAS HOWLING. THE DOORS OF THE DESERT REFUGE, cowering in fear, beat against their own frames. The shuttered windows kept some of the phantoms out and others in, while the wind lashed at them angrily. Resigned, the wind would pretend to leave, only to return with renewed fury. The window frames creaked in vain attempts to free themselves.

Valentín heard footsteps outside, dismal and abandoned. His men were huddled in the drifting snow, the cold sneaking in everywhere, trying to make up for the rest of the day when it was locked away, hungry. The men couldn't even see each other in the black night. The desert had woven itself into the darkness.

Valentín lit a cigar from the flame of his kerosene lamp and breathed out a cloud of smoke. He poured himself a glass of wine. *One day, everyone you ever killed will come back to haunt you, Valentín Cobelo.* So went the curse of a grieving widow years ago. "Do you think so?" he had responded. "What if I told you they are already with me, that I know their footsteps and their shouts? Come with me into the desert at night, doña, that's where they are."

The dead don't leave while we are still thinking about them, Valentín thought. No one leaves them in peace. They wander, tormented, none daring to break their chains. *Who are your dead, Rosario? Are you still shackled to them too?*

A gust of wind finally managed to force itself in, blowing open a shuttered window. The lamp flame faltered. Valentín stood, the wind's needles piercing his face, and latched the window.

What if I died? What if someone killed me? I'd wander around in your memory, afraid that you would forget me, forever aching to touch you again. Another curse like those made every day out here. But who has time to worry about them? I'm not going to die. Death is on my side.

Who are your dead, Rosario? I have seen the face of death, and it will never leave me.

It had been warm, even so late in the evening. There was a light on in his father's study. The light threw shadows on the ground outside the room. His spurs in his hand, Valentín crept closer without making a sound. He saw his father on his knees, crying, begging for mercy, pleading with three of his own men not to kill him. He promised to give them the ranch and everything in it if they would let him go. Only God knows if he yelled for help; no one came. Bent over, sobbing, don Valentín Cobelo Garamendi didn't know his son was watching through the window.

They're going to kill you, Father. Can't you see how much they enjoy hearing you cry? They want to draw out the pleasure of watching you humiliate yourself. No one would believe that it's you in there. What happened to your arrogance? Stop crying! I hate you now more than ever. I can't even remember when I started hating you. It's as if the hatred inside me has strangled everything else, even my memories. And this is how I will always remember you, on your knees, pleading.

They put an end to the pleas with their machetes. Don Valentín Cobelo was cut into pieces, contorted in his own blood, no longer casting his long shadow on the wall.

Out of breath, sweating, veins bulging, the three men stared incredulously at their patrón. They were repulsed by the bloody mess, the scattered flesh. Valentín called out to them, waking them from their stupor. They had barely turned toward him when they felt the heat of his bullets burning their chests, their faces, their legs, until they also were dead.

Up close, it was difficult for Valentín to discern what blood belonged to whom. His boots were stained with it. He stared at his father's disfigured face, nearly cut in two. He felt twinges of pity and contempt.

Cipriano was the first to arrive.

"Did you know about this?" asked Valentín.

"Some."

"Look at all the blood, the eyes, the open mouths. I am going to die when I want to, Cipriano."

"Some people manage it. But death is clever. It hunts down those who don't fear it."

"Come on, let's burn all this. I don't want to leave anything standing."

"Whatever you want, muchacho."

The wind whirled and flung itself against the walls of the houses in the desert refuge. Valentín heard its lashes, its whimpers.

Rosario, when I saw my father lying on the floor, it was as if he had been there forever. I forgot about his life. Suddenly, the waiting was over. That's how it will be for us.

When? When? Rosario asked herself as she stood by the parlor window, heart pounding, staring blankly down the dark street. Anyone passing by and seeing her, in her white nightgown and long straight hair, would think she was a ghost. But no one came by. Only the soft wind blowing in from the desert, and it was accustomed to such visions. No one ever saw her on those lonely nights when she would suddenly awaken, feeling he was coming for her. She would hear the sound of his horse's hooves. But they always passed by before she made it down the stairs, carrying her ability to sleep with it.

"During the day it's easier to bear things, Mamá."

"That's right. During the night you can't distract loneliness."

"Or anything else, for that matter."

"Just stop thinking about the same thing, hija. We should go away for a while. Maybe that would help you forget."

"Go where? I don't want to forget. I just want to know when he's coming back. I want to know what I will feel when he comes back. Sometimes I imagine that I'll die without realizing it; then I'd never know. That's what I used to think years ago, when I thought Papá was coming back. I'd imagine that I'd die and then he'd come back."

"Don't torture yourself, Rosario. God will take care of it."

People are saying they saw him in La Drema with his men, heading up to Los Esquites. They say that since he left Monreal he's been holed up on his hacienda, which is bigger than a whole town; he's probably still there. They say he killed all those people for no reason, because he's a murderer. No one's seen him lately, but that's a bad sign, because they think that means he'll be here any minute. They say he's got women to hide him, but who knows? They even say he killed his father, cut him up with a machete. *Virgen Santa,* Holy Virgin Mary! God protect us! I'm telling you that man is so terrible, I can't repeat all the things they say. They say he's in Valcristo and won't let people out of their houses. They're dying closed up in that heat. But what would he be doing so far away? It's just what I've heard. They're sure he'll go back to Monreal, because he's got this woman there; he made her a widow, can you imagine? They told me his father rides with him, telling him who to kill. I don't believe any of it, but if you ask me I think he'll be back. At least that's what people say.

"Let's head down to Alquemiras, Cipriano. I need a woman. My nerves are getting to me. I want to see Basilia Liu."

Not even a revolution could reduce the number of clients who frequented Basilia Liu's house. A Chinese mestiza from Sonora, she had run away from the smell of dye and spices at an early age, distancing herself from a future bound up in immigrant tradition and the marginalization imposed on anyone slightly different. With only her charm to offer, she set out looking for her fortune.

Her clients thought the Chinese heritage accounted for her discretion. She never talked about the governors, mayors, military chiefs, rich landowners, and bishops who passed along her busy hallways. She never allowed conspiracy, and there had never been a murder or an act of revenge in her house.

Only pleasure was allowed in La Casa de Basilia Liu. She believed every man had a right to a moment of happiness, without judgment, conditions, or demands. She simply kept the sad stories she was told to herself. She did not allow her girls to walk naked in the halls or parlors, although they were encouraged to show cleavage to entice and stimulate the clientele. She taught them how to share secrets and recite the poets Bécquer and Campoamor.

Her canapés were exquisite. Her sofas were Queen Anne, but the bedrooms were strictly Victorian. Paintings and drawings by Leandro Izaguirre and Jean Bernard adorned the walls, depicting scenes of merriment and romance, images of languid robust women adorned with roses, magnolias, and narcissus. Drinks were poured from Bohemian crystal carafes into Murano glasses. She was quick to charge clients for breakage.

Only three men ever died in her house. Don Celodia de la Garza never let a week pass (in later years it was a month) without locking himself in a room with two giggling women. Finally at age seventy, smothered by caresses, pomades, and body oils, he closed his eyes for the last time just at the joyously anticipated moment of pleasure.

A few years before, don Justino Villafuerte, sitting on a cushion, brought his hand to his chest and died suddenly in a fit of laughter induced by a sensuous and malicious tongue.

The third casualty, a young man with an admittedly weak heart, died of love for his wife to be. He had come to Basilia Liu's house to prepare himself for his duties on the upcoming wedding night.

Basilia ingeniously arranged for friends to take the dead men to their homes with carefully crafted stories about the circumstances of their unfortunate deaths.

Basilia had heeded an inner call to become a madam. She was so proud of this that no one ever doubted her. No one ever heard her complain about her life, or about any unfulfilled passions eating away at her. She was a magnificent and generous woman.

One night she took Valentín Cobelo under her wing. He had just turned twenty and was quiet and docile. She taught him about secret places in the skin and the hidden pleasures of the flesh. "Put your hand here, then move the other like this, gently. Run your mouth along here, releasing your breath, warming the skin. Then press your fingers here and caress this part with your whole hand. Slowly, Valentín, slowly. It only gets better. Few men know that, and even fewer really understand it. To have more, you have to give more. You have to surrender unconditionally. You don't have to love. It's enough to know what you want to feel. Not many men know that either. Don't forget, it's not something to rush through. You have to believe it will never end, like agony."

She liked him and enjoyed teaching him, but she was always searching for him beyond the few words he spoke. She looked into his eyes, trying to figure out when his soul had been wrenched out of him.

After she turned thirty-five, Basilia Liu never again slept with Valentín or any other man. She thought men should be given everything in good order, and when things started moving around more than they should, one had to be considerate enough not to try and fool them.

Valentín Cobelo was not a steady customer, and he always tried to avoid other clients, preferring to have the house at his and his men's complete disposal. After Basilia stopped sleeping with him, he never slept with the same woman twice. Some forgot him, others never could, but none of them had ever seen a man like him before. He never spoke, but he was capable of making them feel such ecstasy that it seemed as if he were promising to love them with the same intensity for the rest of their lives. When he returned to Basilia's house, if a woman he had been with before was still there, she was less than a shadow to him. He never looked at her again.

Once Basilia Liu sent him a beautiful *morenita* who had just escaped the chains of poverty in Jalisco. She was nearly fifteen, with eyes like moist almonds, and she was the only one that Valentín Cobelo ever spoke to. He told her she was still a little girl, too young for this sort of work. *You are beautiful and have your whole life ahead of you.* Then he told Basilia Liu he didn't like new girls, didn't want to break them in. After that, Basilia Liu never sent him a woman younger than twenty, and certainly no virgins.

Basilia Liu wondered what brought him there that night with Cipriano, Julián Vela, and Rarámuri. She gave him a quiet, comforting smile and two bottles of the wine she always kept for him.

While Valentín was in Basilia Liu's house, no one was allowed to enter or exit. No music played. The women who were not chosen were told to go to their rooms and turn out their lights. No talking was allowed.

Miguel, Basilia's bartender from the beginning, brought over two glasses and some cheese.

"How are you, don Miguel?" asked Valentín.

"The same, señor. Can you believe I just turned ninety and still have enough strength for a woman? But, doña Basilia won't let me."

"I just don't want you to die on me, Miguel, that's all."

"But I can still do it. Excuse me."

Valentín liked it when Basilia sat with him. They spoke very little, but they understood each other and could feel what the other was thinking without even touching. Sometimes she would bring out the Spanish playing cards and make up stories about the king of gold and his hatred of the king of swords. She told him how the queen of clubs meddled in the affairs of the knight of cups, who was the only one capable of breaking the spell cast on her by the ace of clubs.

Basilia Liu was knowledgeable about card reading, but she had never read Valentín's fortune. Sometimes he let her look at the lines in his hand, but she never read them; she simply told him what each one represented.

This time Valentín barely listened to Basilia Liu as he finished the first bottle of wine. She watched him closely as she chatted about the knight of swords and the queen of gold.

"So the tornado has finally hit your shores, Valentín."

"A woman."

"Look, Valentín, you're not made for love."

"But I feel it, Basilia."

"No doubt, but I'm not sure how. I wouldn't want to be her."

The terrified shrieks of a woman upstairs interrupted them. A young woman approached Basilia Liu and told her she could not stand the man she was with; he was an Indio. She pleaded for someone else to take her place. Rarámuri crouched on the balcony above, saying nothing.

Valentín took the woman's arm.

"You take care of him or I'll kill you."

The woman's fear intensified. She was too frightened to speak. Tears formed at the corners of her eyes. Basilia softly asked her to go back to him, and she did, swallowing her protests and pushing them back down her throat as she reluctantly climbed the stairs.

"Valentín, that man is really scary."

"He's just a man. He would give his life for me."

It went back to a day in Pizoarillo. Valentín had just arrived in the little pueblo with Cipriano, Serafín Machuca, Julián Vela, and a few other men. In the main square, a group of local police had an Indian tied to the backside of a horse. They were drinking mescal and laughing as they took turns raping his wife at knifepoint.

"Let's kill these idiots," said Valentín. "But leave the one on the woman for the man to take care of." At his command, his men shot at the arms and legs of the rural police. Julián Vela pulled out his knife and planted it squarely in the chest of the man holding the bottle of mescal to his mouth, instantly filling it with blood. As soon as the policemen realized what was happening, Valentín and his men drew nearer, shooting to kill.

The one they had temporarily spared moved away from the woman, dragging himself across the ground and staring at his assailants as they approached. Cipriano untied the captive and offered him his rifle. The Indian wouldn't take it. He reached for Julián's knife instead. He walked over to his wife, who had already died without the policeman noticing. The frightened man tried to run, but Valentín grabbed him by the collar. The policeman desperately reached for his gun. The Indian threw the knife, piercing his hand, then jumped on him, removed the knife, and stabbed him in the chest with a twisting motion. As the policeman's blood splashed on his attacker's face, the last thing he saw was the knife driven into his mouth.

The Indian stood up and stared at his hands for a few seconds. He walked over to the water trough and splashed water on his hands and face. Then he went over to his wife and gently pulled down her skirt. Without a sound he buried his face in her bosom. It was still warm. He picked her up carefully, like a sleeping child, turned silently, and carried her away.

Serafín looked at the policemen's bodies. He saw one about his own size and picked up a gray jacket and threw it over his shoulder. They took all the weapons. The few curious onlookers dispersed quickly, leaving the bodies where they had fallen.

Later that evening, as Valentín and his men ate around their fire on the edge of the desert, the Indian approached, bareback on a horse. Valentín watched the man dismount and come toward him. "You are my Rarámuri, my leader," he said, as he cut open his arm and offered it. Valentín did the same. Then they all returned to Pizoarillo and burned it to the ground. As the townspeople ran half naked into the street, Valentín Cobelo and his men shot them to punish them for their cowardice.

After a while, Rarámuri descended the stairs with the woman who had cried out in terror not long before. She was now hugging his waist, her face covered by her hair. They sat down together at a table.

"I'm going upstairs, Basilia. Send up the one with the doe eyes."

"Why don't you take her with you?"

"Just send her up. I'll wait for her upstairs."

Rosario. Rosario. Rosario. He saw her, felt her, ran his hands over her body, covered her with his breath. Rosario became the woman there with him in that dark, hot, dry room. The woman with the doe eyes, nameless and unknown, lay among the silk sheets with embroidered flowers, not realizing that she had become another woman, that her sighs were no longer her own, that the pleasure she was given was not hers.

Rosario was suddenly awakened in the darkness of her room, an intense desire possessing her entire body, making her short of breath and bathing her in a glistening sweat. She saw Valentín Cobelo gazing into her eyes and was filled with fear. Then, abruptly, he was gone, leaving her alone, with sleeplessness for company.

She sat up in bed and took a deep breath. Her nightgown and the back of her neck were soaking wet, her breasts ached, and her thighs were boiling. She lay back on the bed, tossing the sheets aside, and began caressing her body, afraid to close her eyes again.

Silently, Valentín laid his hand over her eyelids, as one would do for someone who had died. The young woman understood that he didn't want her to look at him. As his mind traveled she granted him freedom, becoming nothing more than a body, a woman far away.

Rosario, her desire now wrung out of her, covered herself again with the sheets to hide her loneliness. Valentín reined in his wandering mind. Both fell asleep, without the other to hold.

SEVEN

"WHY DON'T YOU TALK WITH FATHER IGNACIO? MAYBE HE CAN give you some advice," Severina suggested, without looking up from her crocheting.

"Advice from a priest?" Rosario threw her embroidery hoops to the floor. "And from Father Ignacio, at that! The poor man can't even look me in the eye, he gets so nervous when I speak to him. Is he shy, or could there be another reason?"

"Por Dios, Rosario!"

"What could a priest tell me about these things? He would only say that it's part of God's design and I must submit to His will. Indeed! Then he would ask me to confess. He would say that the devil takes a million different forms to tempt us to sin. I really can't see a priest having anything useful to say."

"Rosario, don't be so arrogant."

"I'm not being arrogant. But I'm not naive either."

"You haven't asked for advice, but I'm going to give you some anyway, Valentín," said Basilia, as she took his face in her hands. "Stop trying to fool yourself. Women can wait forever for something. Time is different for us. But a man must be careful. He could be too late or too soon."

Once long ago, feeling lost and uncertain, Rosario Alomar had told her mother that she wanted to ask Castalia Leguado to reveal the future. "I've already gone to see her, hija," Severina replied, "and she assured me that your father would never return, though she couldn't tell me whether or not he was dead. I think it's better for us to believe he is." And so Rosario did.

Now she was drawn to doña Castalia by sleepless nights and an overwrought imagination. She went secretly, hoping for a few words that would bring her closer to the quiet river of peace or the deep pool of certainty. She desperately needed something tangible to believe in.

Her anxiety was so overpowering that the mere sight of the fortune-teller was enough to calm her.

Castalia Leguado had not been out of her house in twenty years. She wanted to stay out of the way of a former client who, after everything she foretold came to pass, threatened to kill her the next time she saw her on the street. She lifted her head of fluffy white hair, like a distant mountaintop. Her beady eyes peered from the web of wrinkles surrounding them.

"You have finally come. No one can live very long without wanting to know what is ahead or what has already gone by unnoticed. I have heard so much about you that I had begun to think you were not real. And now look. Here you are.

"You are restless. Nothing can hold you in one place. I see that you want to run far away, but when you get there you want to be somewhere else. Even in your sleep you cannot be still. I see it in your face. You're lost in the forest of uncertain love. Your mother was not like this. She came to me once and went away with a truth so big she never came back. Maybe it will be that way with you too.

"Shuffle the cards seven times and concentrate on what you want to know. You are even more lovely than I imagined. But it's not good to be so beautiful. It almost always leads to misfortune. It draws envy. Men desire beautiful women and want to be with them, but then they are so dazzled they can't see the woman for herself and can never really love her. Men are attracted by beauty, but they do not trust beautiful women. They think such women are deceitful. You must remember this. But I can see you are a woman to be reckoned with.

"Cut the cards into two stacks. Don't allow your hands to tremble, otherwise destiny becomes ruthless; it cannot forgive fear. Place your hand on top of the cards—no, the left hand. You have very strong hands. Close your eyes and repeat after me, 'For me, for my home, for what awaits me.' "

Rosario repeated the words.

"Now ask the question in your mind and put the full power of your faith in the cards. Don't be afraid. What is going to happen will happen regardless. But now you will know ahead of time, even if right up until that moment you don't believe it. The cards don't lie."

Doña Castalia began laying out the cards, veins like green rivers running over the backs of her wrinkled hands. Two rows of five cards each, face down. Twenty more cards on top of the first ones. Before she laid the last ten, she warned Rosario that if the four aces appeared it meant yes and if they didn't it meant no. If three show up, it will take a while, but yes. She laid the final ten cards face up. The seven of swords. The queen of clubs. The first ace, of swords. Two of gold. Knight of swords. The ace of clubs. Six of clubs. The ace of cups. The three of swords. And the ace of gold.

Castalia Leguado let out a scratchy laugh. Rosario wiped her hands on her skirt, wet her lips, and said, "He'll be back then?" Doña Castalia assured her that he would, without a doubt, be back.

"He is a man without a woman. He is on another path, debating with himself. At first, when he appears at your door, his return will bring you much happiness. But he is a powerful and dangerous man. Do you want to see what is in the other cards?"

Rosario thought of continuing but decided against it. "Just tell me how long it will be before he comes back."

Doña Castalia studied the upturned cards once more to make sure she had not missed anything. "It won't be today or tomorrow, but when you least expect it and sooner than you had imagined. Worry will only cause delay."

As she left doña Castalia's house, Rosario was greeted by a glorious sun. There was no hint of a breeze, but the heat felt good on her body. She walked confidently, aglow with tranquillity and hope. The Valdepeña brothers smiled at her and touched their hats as she passed. Doña Celedonia Santos asked about Severina, saying she was surprised not to have seen her at church. At don Crescencio's fabric store she bought taffeta, flannel, silk thread, and both black and pink beads.

Back on the street, the sun gallantly escorted her on her way. She was happy she had worn a cotton dress and flat shoes. Later she would tell her mother how doña Ernestina Ezpilcueta and her daughter María, who bragged so about being Basque, not Spanish, and were really nothing more than shoe-selling *gachupina,* had pretended not to see her leave don Eleuterio's store so they wouldn't have to say hello. Don Eleuterio, whose only son had died in the recent skirmish, had also been brusque with her. But she ignored it and bought seed for the canaries, some flour and beans, nothing else, because it made for a rather heavy bundle and she hadn't brought a bag. She had forgotten the glycerin soap and bubble bath, but she could get them tomorrow. Monreal looked clean after the rain. The houses and the earth shone brilliantly in the sun. Even the shadows gleamed. Except for the six-thirty rosary, no one would suspect that this tranquil town had recently been the site of a fratricidal bloodbath.

When she returned home, Rosario Alomar found don Victoriano Gómez Calleja and his wife waiting for her. Impeccably mannered, they were embarrassed at having to visit during such a difficult time, but they were seeking the deed for a house in Coauchapa that señor don Federico, may he rest in peace, had been kind enough to offer to draw up for them. They had already paid an advance equal to the amount shown on the receipt that they now held out to Rosario.

She thanked them for their understanding and said that, yes, it was a difficult time, but life must continue. She promised to have the papers ready the following day and went on to ask them to tell anyone else who might have entrusted something to Federico that she intended, as much as possible, to bring such business to a close.

Don Victoriano and his wife, Felícitas Menchaca, in whose name the deed was to be drawn up, thanked Rosario for her kindness and asked if they might come back at five o'clock the following afternoon. She told them it would be fine.

Rosario entered Federico's study. She opened the rolltop desk and started going through his papers, opening and closing drawers. Gold-tipped Bakelite pens, navy, black, and purple inkwells, notebooks with red, green, and purple ties. She touched everything gently, carefully. She found his seal, Federico Farías Calda, lawyer, notary public of Monreal. The black ink pad. She also found, half completed, the deed that had been solicited, some notes detailing the granting of another property, don Guadalupe Herrería's unfinished will, a file of clippings from newspapers and political magazines, and some political flyers. She pulled the autographed copy of *The Presidential Succession* from its nook, dedicated *To don Federico Farías, a man of noble democratic ideals. Affectionately yours, your friend, Francisco I. Madero.* Rosario smiled to herself, feeling a surge of bittersweet excitement.

She sat down and began to examine each of the documents carefully. Rather than becoming absorbed in his work, Rosario felt her husband growing closer to her physically and emotionally until he seemed to be there with her. It was as if he had come back to remind her of his goodness, his unwavering love for her, his understanding and compassion about her not being able to have children. She was reminded of his dream of a just and empowered country and of the countless letters he wrote to the ministers of war in Spain and Cuba in an attempt to verify what had really happened to don Celestino. Rosario wept softly, allowing her thoughts to embrace her husband, who had loved her so properly.

Doña Severina heard the now-familiar sound of Rosario's

grief. She looked in the room and saw her daughter crying at the desk, papers in hand, and left quietly, holding back her own sorrow, not wanting to intrude.

Rosario wiped away her tears, dipped the pen in the blue inkwell, and set about finishing the deed for the house in Coauchapa, exactly as Federico had taught her. She paid special attention to her calligraphy, which her husband had so admired, wanting to ensure that her work honored the seal of the notary public of Monreal.

Valentín and Cipriano rode in the desert for several hours, regarding their domain while the fierce sun watched over them. Here between sun and earth their horses stepped firmly, binding them to this land but also giving them freedom.

They liked the silence of this oven, a silence they trampled with each step. Every sound had its own fleeting moment. The tarantula's abrupt, violent movements, the puma's cautious tread, the vulture's cynical flutter of wings, even the snake's treacherous slither. Only the silence and the land remained immutable, insatiable; even the sun came and went, pushed out by evening, rushing to embrace the new day.

They were on their way to El Faro, a desolate, meager hill from which they could look over the expanse before them. It was a world of parched earth, rocks, yuccas, and cacti, open and blindingly scorching by day, cold and sheathed in black by night. They knew the many faces and masks of this land, had seen them all during nights of ferocious winds and days of bitter heat.

Cipriano had named El Faro after a seascape that had hung in Valentín's father's parlor. It was the painting of a lone lighthouse, standing proud and stubborn above the waves of an angry sea. Valentín thought the hill was a perfect place to regard the horizon, no longer a seashore but just as violent.

Sweating and out of breath, his mouth completely dry, Valentín looked down from El Faro, staring out over his vast, unconquered land. No one had given it to him, and certainly no one could ever take it away.

"How long have we been coming out here, Cipriano?"

"Ay, muchacho, you were just a boy. Your soul was just starting to awaken."

"Basilia is still wondering when my soul was removed."

"That's a woman for you. Nobody took it, you just changed. When a snake grows out of its old skin, it has a new skin underneath."

Valentín took a couple of swigs of the *tesgüiño* Rarámuri had given them. Cipriano rolled a cigarette. Far away, where the desert drew closer to the sky, a white strip of sunlight shimmered.

"I don't know why I've got death on my mind," said Valentín in a hushed voice, as if his thoughts had escaped and galloped away with his words.

"You're afraid of dying. I was like that before Fidelia died. Her death took the fear away. After everything else is gone, only death remains." Cipriano raised his head to look at Valentín directly. Their eyes met for a moment; then Valentín looked back out over the desert.

"Maybe I am afraid, but I'm not sure it's worth the trouble."

"Who knows? If you fear death as it approaches, you're lost. If not, if you can look her in the face and conquer her, she'll back off, but she'll keep her eye on you. That's when she's at her worst, when she's stalking you, testing you."

Very slowly, Valentín pulled out his machete. Cipriano,

understanding, kept still. In one swift move, Valentín swung the machete and hacked off the head of a snake preparing to strike Cipriano.

"You caught the poor thing off guard, boy."

"She was hypnotized by all the talking."

Their laughter flowed like a spring in the dry desert.

Serafín Machuca had heard that a military train carrying three thousand pesos in gold was passing through Coauchapa on its way to the United States to buy weapons.

"It's not that easy," said Cipriano, when he heard the plan Serafín had laid out. "You forgot about the machine guns. We can take care of the federales, but the machine guns are another story."

"Do you want that gold, Serafín? Jerónimo?" Valentín was looking at them. He didn't wait for them to respond. "I think the others want it too."

"It's risky. I don't think we should do it. That train is too well equipped."

Valentín concealed the irritation and impatience caused by Cipriano's words. "I know we can do it. Where is the best place to strike?"

"There are some rocky hills near Coauchapa. With a little dynamite we could cover the tracks with rocks, but they'd expect an attack there," offered Jerónimo Pastor, who knew the area well.

"It's the most logical spot, right? So that means anybody else with the same idea would think of attacking there too. Isn't there another place?"

"There's the Coasalita bridge over the Culebras River. We could blow it up. Nobody would think of doing that because everybody uses it, federales, revolucionarios; otherwise you have to go all the way up to Manzanares," explained Jerónimo.

"We could do it, boss," said Serafín Machuca, "but I don't know about those damned machine guns. Our cannons are nothing next to them. You saw how it was in Alamilla. I should've grabbed us one."

"Are you scared, Serafín?" Valentín was taunting him. He knew he had the last word, but he wanted to be sure of Serafín's absolute commitment, wanted him to fight out of desire, not just because he was ordered to.

"Damn it! You really want to do it? Let's go, then! You know you can count on me, the others too. Who doesn't like a little gold?"

"Okay, let's go up to Coasalita then. It's gonna be a hell of a job."

"Yeah, we'd better get going. It'll take us awhile to get there."

"We can make it in two days if we keep a good pace," said Jerónimo.

"Let's get ready. We'll be taking just about everybody. Where's Julián?"

"He went off with Rarámuri to learn about plants. They shouldn't be long," said Cipriano.

"We'll leave when they get back."

Jerónimo and Serafín went outside and starting yelling for everybody to get ready. The men made preparations to leave without asking why or where they were going. They followed orders. They adjusted bandoliers, sharpened machetes, filled water bags, and saddled horses without a sense of either fear or expectation.

"Do you really care about the gold, muchacho? No one's challenging you."

"I have to do it."

"Let's hope luck is on our side."

They rode all day, stopping only to rub their horses' legs and let them drink. As darkness approached, they set up camp near Monreal.

After a few cups of coffee and a two shots of *tesgüino*, Valentín lay back against his saddle, contemplating nightfall.

The men unloaded their weapons as if arriving home after a hard day's work. Only a trace of the sun's heat lingered. Flames from the cooking fires lapped serenely at the sky.

A voluptuous moon graced the young night. The stars seemed as if they might fall out of the sky at any moment.

"Close enough to grab and throw among the dry branches to brighten up the fire, don't you think, Cipriano?" asked Valentín.

"Yeah. Doesn't it feel sometimes like we're riding up there with them?"

"Yes. Sometimes I let my thoughts wander, not going anywhere in particular, riding around in the night."

"Exactly. You don't want morning to break, because then the sun comes along and says you have to be going somewhere definite. You can't just stand there without direction or purpose."

"You feel the sun, but you can only look at the stars. They command you to look at them," said Valentín.

"I don't understand people who lock themselves inside the minute night falls. They don't know how different the earth smells at night."

"I can never sleep on nights like this, even when I'm exhausted. I know the night will abandon me if I fall asleep; I have to court her so I can enjoy her company a little more."

"It would be great not to have to sleep. I think that's why older people like me don't sleep much. It's as if something inside you says, *You are going to die soon. Open your eyes and look at everything now, because soon you won't be able to.* I don't want to die in my sleep. I would feel betrayed by life."

"You're not old enough to sleep so little, Cipriano."

"Then maybe I'm going to die soon."

"Do you think we know when we're going to die?"

"Only God knows."

They stopped talking and lay there quietly traveling through the stars, each off in his own direction, exploring, wandering.

"I'm going for a ride. Want to come?" asked Valentín.

"What for? You go alone."

They shared a knowing smile. Rarámuri saw Valentín preparing his horse and was about to offer to go with him. Cipriano stopped him.

"Let him go. He's not risking his life. He'll be back soon."

Valentín Cobelo arrived at Rosario Alomar's home, lit only by a gas lamp over the front door. Not daring to dismount, he stopped and stared at the house. The only sound was the occasional barking of a dog in the distance. A warm, soft breeze blew from the south.

If you only knew that I am here, that I need to see you. You're up there sleeping, not knowing where I am. Wake up, Rosario. I don't want to make a mistake and find out that it's too late.

Rosario woke up, startled. She didn't want to run to the window as she had every other night, only to be disappointed. But this time the sound of horses' hooves had stopped right in front of the house. She held her breath and cleared her mind, focusing her attention on the sensations running through her blood, beating in her heart, telling her it was him. He had arrived.

Valentín wanted to look through those walls to see Rosario. In his mind, he saw her again as she turned and walked through the door. He saw her disappear into the house.

I know you are in there, Rosario. You haven't gone away. I can smell you. This house is full of you. On my way here I felt I was discovering something I had dreamed about, and with each step I took, my dream came closer to reality. I know you are in there.

Without understanding why, Rosario forced herself not to go to the window. If he called her, she wouldn't be able to control herself. She felt like an animal in a cave, waiting, her mate circling outside, sniffing to make sure she was still there, still alive, then returning to the hills to resume the hunt.

If I see you, talk to you, I won't be able to leave without you, Rosario. Tonight you could conquer me, own me.

Valentín, you came back! Don't say anything, not tonight. I'm still afraid. Why didn't you take me away last time? Why did you leave me here, to think only about you?

Rosario tried to slow the racing of her nervous heart and listen to the silence that had brought Valentín Cobelo to her.

The temptation is getting stronger, Rosario. Today I thought we would run away and leave all this behind, but it was just a dream.

Valentín pulled lightly on the reins and turned his horse back toward camp.

When she heard the sound of hooves hitting the street, Rosario sat up in bed. Had it really been Valentín? Afraid she was imagining things again, although she could still hear his horse, she went to the window and lit a lamp. The abruptness of the flame called out to Valentín, and he turned back for a moment. In that instant they both knew it was real. A warm joy evaporated their sadness and comforted them as Valentín continued on his way.

Rosario watched him until he was out of sight and returned to her bed, confident that her wait was over. Maybe tomorrow, she thought, smiling.

"It's true, Cipriano," he said, his eyes shining brightly. "She's waiting for me, I know she is."

"You sound just like a little kid."

EIGHT

RISING UP OVER THE NEARLY DRY CULEBRAS RIVER, THE BRIDGE was no more than three hundred feet across. In some places the river flowed happily along, but in others it was the mere memory of a river. For a few months each year, though, it ran peacefully and clear.

The men set up camp several hundred yards from the bridge, amid the green-gray trees and the dry, thorny brush.

Valentín rode over to the bridge with Julián and Serafín. Serafín opened his mouth to speak, but Valentín stopped him with a wave of his hand. He didn't want to hear any sounds other than those natural to the area. He was absorbing the land, the surroundings, and the bridge. Valentín approached, stopping to examine the bridge carefully, then rode slowly over it, listening to the sounds his horse's hooves made on the creaking wood. He inspected the connections that held the beams together, studied how the rail ties were attached, and counted the main steel posts. Julián and Serafín followed Valentín in silence, watching, waiting for him to say something.

He retraced his steps, alternating his gaze between the horizon from where the train would approach and the structure itself. When he reached the other end of the bridge, he crossed to the other side and returned. He called for Jerónimo, Rarámuri, and Cipriano.

"It'll be easy to blow up," he said finally, "but we'll need to be precise."

"We don't have a remote detonator, General," reported Serafín.

"Then some of the men will have to use bundles of dynamite with long fuses. Julián will signal them when to light the fuses; then they'll climb down the supports and race away."

"Before the train gets there?" asked Jerónimo.

"No, we have to detonate just as the engine crosses the bridge. When it falls it'll drag two or three other cars with it."

"The gold is probably in one of the middle cars. That's where they carried it when I was in the rural police," said Serafín.

"The explosion will catch them by surprise, so we won't have to fight the federales."

"Where do you want the rest of the men?" Cipriano asked.

"We'll put about eighty of them a few hundred feet away from the tracks. They're to wait until the federales appear after the explosion and then start shooting. Once the fighting begins, the rest of us will join you and spread out along the tracks."

"What about the machine guns?"

"Serafín, you assign some men to take care of them. The rest of us will provide cover. Have them try to save one for us and blow up the rest."

"What if the signal fails or the bridge doesn't go up at the right time?" Cipriano looked at Valentín.

"We'd better do it right, or all hell's gonna break out."

"Well, then, may God be on our side, General," said Julián Vela.

"Go ahead and pray, but don't let it distract you," said Valentín.

Ten men were positioned along the span. Each one had placed packages of dynamite attached to long fuses, which they held gingerly. As the minutes passed, their sweat grew stickier and more profuse. It rolled down their bodies while impatience twisted their tortured nerves. Alert and attentive, they waited for Julián's signal. Before long, they began to feel slight, barely perceptible vibrations in the beams on which they sat. The train was drawing near. Instinctively, they glanced at the ropes they had prepared to slide down and escape the explosion. They still could not see the train, but the vibrations were growing stronger. Anxiously awaiting his signal, they stared at Julián Vela, the vibrations now seeping into their muscles and bones. Still no signal.

From a distance, Valentín motioned to Julián, but Julián saw nothing but the approaching locomotive. Serafín, lying in the dirt with his men, looked at the train, then at Julián, and shouted at Julián. Bound together by despair, the men on the bridge lit their fuses, not even noticing that Julián was signaling to them that very instant. They slid down the ropes frantically, burning their hands and tearing deep gashes in them. Thinking only of getting as far away as possible before the explosion, some of the men let go and fell into the water below.

As they heard the blast the others dropped to the ground to protect themselves from flying debris, which soared into the air only to drop like tired birds. The engine plunged into the riverbed, pulling the coal wagon and the first passenger car of federales with it. The rest of the cars stopped short of the collapsed bridge. Serafín and his men started shooting. They soon found out that there were machine guns, not only on top of three of the cars but inside them as well. Placed at the windows, the guns spit bullets in all directions. Bullets saturated the ground, which Serafín and his men were supposed to be covering. They wished the earth would swallow them, provide cover from the rain of bullets that held them captive. If they lifted their heads even the slightest bit, they would be killed instantly.

Sandbags protected the soldiers working the machine guns on the roofs of the train cars, making it impossible to see the gunmen, but they generated a deafening noise and a deadly stream of metal nonetheless. The revolving guns spun like the heads of angry snakes. Serafín Machuca thought it was useless to try to conquer his fear. Bravery would be a waste of energy. Instead, he closed his eyes, hoping the resulting darkness would make the time pass more quickly. If he didn't see the bullets, maybe they wouldn't see him. He and his men couldn't even back up, let alone retreat. They were hemmed in by death.

At a distance, impatient and furious, all thought blurred by the images in front of him, Valentín Cobelo sought a moment, a split second of respite in which to give his men the order to attack.

"They're gonna get killed, muchacho!"

"I'm thinking, Cipriano! I'm in the same hole they are!"

"You better make this damn massacre serve some purpose! Or let's go die with them."

"Rarámuri! Jerónimo! Take a couple of men with you and climb up that hanging car. Crawl under the cars until you get to the three with machine guns. Put bundles of dynamite under their wheels, light the fuses, and get back out."

When they reached the river, Jerónimo and Rarámuri heard an explosion. Julián and Serafín had tried to throw some dynamite at the train. The explosives had fallen short, killing half their men.

Jerónimo and Ceferino crawled under the last car armed with machine guns and placed their bundles. Rarámuri and Filiberto carefully placed dynamite under the other two. Jerónimo and Ceferino lit the fuses in sequence, crawling backwards, afraid to look up. There was no time to think about failure. They didn't stop when they heard the first car blow. They reached the last car just as the second one exploded, and then they scrambled for their lives. Under the engine, lying in the riverbed, they paused to realize that they were still alive. Ceferino cried and clawed at the dry earth between the bodies littering the ground until his hands bled.

Valentín Cobelo galloped maniacally toward the train, machete in one hand, rifle in the other, eager to unleash his fury, ready to destroy.

Federales were already jumping out of the windows when the new explosions erupted. Free to move at last, Julián and Serafín's men charged toward the train, shooting and yelling as they ran.

Valentín raced along the side of the train, dodging bullets and using his machete to cut the heads off any federales he could find. A federal officer saw him approach, grabbed his rifle in both hands, and shot him, knocking him off his horse. Biting down on his pain and feeling warm blood gushing out of his chest, Valentín struggled to his feet and searched for his assailant. His vision blurred, which infuriated him further. Over and over he fired his gun. Rivers of sweat were pouring down his face and neck, mingling with his blood. The air boiled, choking him. He shot again just as another bullet entered his thigh, causing him to double over in pain. His body, gushing blood, refused to move. He could not get up. He was going to die. Still obsessed with the man who had shot him, Valentín raised his head. He could barely make out a hunched-over figure moving toward him, holding his stomach with one hand, his rifle with the other, preparing to shoot again. Valentín could feel death lurking nearby, not yet choosing sides but holding out her hand to both men, sucking away their breath. The officer pulled the trigger, but he was out of bullets. He pulled out his saber. Valentín was not afraid of dying. What terrified him was this man stubbornly making his way toward him, coaxed along by death. His legs no longer obeying, Valentín simply stood there, waiting for his opponent to come to him. He couldn't hear anything. Earth, space, life—all was reduced to this man moving toward him, to the distance that separated their bodies. He burned with the need to overcome his fear and keep on living. His vision was completely clouded over with blood, but he shot again at the figure in front of him and saw him fall to the ground. Valentín moved closer and fell to the ground himself. He summoned up enough strength to take the saber from the officer's hand, as the life escaping that other body seeped into his. He ran the saber through the officer's body and kept run-

ning it through his flesh until he collapsed on top of the
bloody corpse, holding on so he wouldn't fall into the vast
darkness of those opaque eyes.

No one heard the last shot. The noon hour was bathed
in indifferent, blinding sunshine, heavy in its own heat. A
slight wind, looking for some other place, began to blow.
Sleepy leaves barely stirred. Corpses and agonized survivors
were spread out over the red, rocky earth. They were so scattered, their moans were barely audible. Valentín Cobelo lay
still.

Smoke rose sluggishly into the sky, moved feebly by the
wind. Men moved from one body to the next among their
compañeros, looking for signs of life, commiserating, reach-
ing out in vain to pleading eyes that closed in a violent heave
of blood in the middle of a half-spoken phrase. Mercilessly,
they picked over the bodies of the federales, searching for
gold chains, medals, money. They tore off belts, boots, and
bandoliers, took rifles and pistols, stabbed any survivors with
a knife or a saber, sliced their throats, or shot them, dizzy with
the smell of blood, overcome by the sensual pleasure of hate.

With river water and *tesgüiño*, Rarámuri bathed Valentín
Cobelo's wounds, then covered them with leaves tied with
strips of leather. The most critical one was on his left side,
though the bleeding had subsided. Valentín's eyes were closed
and he breathed haltingly.

Cipriano crouched beside him. He couldn't speak. There
was nothing to say anyway. Anger, compassion, and tenderness stirred in his heart as he looked at Valentín. Quietly,
Rarámuri tended his wounds, eager to do anything to stave
off his growing feeling of helplessness.

"You got what you wanted, muchacho." Cipriano's voice

was filled with sadness. When his eyes grew teary, he got up and walked away.

Following orders, the men put the bodies of the federales into the train cars that were still more or less intact, piling them up like sacks of grain.

They burned the train. A giant plume of black smoke rose quickly as if to avoid the acrid smell of burning flesh. Frightened by the flames, the crows and vultures screeched curses and flew away.

The casualties from Valentín Cobelo's army were lined up, legs straightened out, arms by their sides, eyes and mouths closed. Cipriano and Valentín had taught the men to respect their dead. Each man had given his life for the group and deserved respect and a proper burial.

They buried the men in individual graves, unmarked by crosses. Then they flattened the ground.

The fires from the train cars were almost burned out. Only here and there were stubborn flames feeding on the twisted cars and the bodies that refused to be consumed. The smell of burned flesh seared the air. The vultures came back.

Valentín's men dragged the gold, in small metal boxes like children's coffins, in among the trees.

The heat showed no sign of subsiding. Valentín was sweating profusely. His head burned like a torch. Rarámuri sprinkled river water on his feet, rubbing them with long triangular leaves.

"Serafín, get the men ready to go. It won't be long before the people in Coauchapa start wondering where the train is and send someone out."

"Where are we taking the general, Cipriano? I think we should head for Monreal."

"No, they'd probably attack us, and we're not ready for another battle. We have to try for La Higareda or at least get deeper into the desert."

Julián came running. "Look!" He pointed to the other side of the railroad tracks. A man on horseback was approaching.

"Don't shoot. He's carrying a white flag," ordered Cipriano.

"Get behind the trees. Prepare for an attack," Serafín yelled to his men. They quickly positioned themselves behind the brush and trees.

"Quick, move Valentín farther in!"

The rider stopped at the tracks.

"General Francisco Larios sent me! He would like to speak with General Valentín Cobelo! We come in peace!"

Cipriano and Serafín Machuca walked toward the man.

"What does he want?"

"I was just sent to deliver the message. I don't know anything else."

"Larios must have been waiting for that train too, Cipriano."

"Looks like it. Come over here." They walked away from the messenger. "We're at a disadvantage and he knows it, but I think we can trust him. If we don't talk to him now, he'll send his men after us. He won't appreciate any discourtesy. Maybe he can help us."

"The bastard wants the gold. We got to it before he could."

"Let's just see what he wants."

They walked back toward the rider.

"Tell General Larios to come here. If anyone comes with him, we'll shoot."

The man rode off.

Serafín kept the men in place. Four of them had fashioned a stretcher for Valentín Cobelo out of branches, strips of leather, and blankets. Rarámuri was off searching for medicinal plants. Valentín's fever was coming down and the sun had reluctantly begun to set, but there were still a few hours until nightfall.

Francisco Larios appeared with his messenger, who was ordered to stop and wait some distance short of the meeting place. He rode up to Cipriano and Serafín Machuca. Julián Vela, who was sitting with Valentín, watched closely.

Larios grew suspicious when he saw that Valentín was not waiting for him. He wasn't sure it was a deliberate display of arrogance, but he found it hard to believe that these men had been sent to represent him. He remained expressionless.

"Good afternoon. I would like to speak with General Cobelo." His tanned, angular face gave added confidence to his words. His request was delivered like an order.

"That's not possible. He is wounded." Cipriano gestured with his head in the general area where Valentín was resting.

Larios expressed open annoyance and surprise. He glanced around. "With all due respect, I would like to see him."

"As you wish."

The three men walked toward Valentín Cobelo. Julián stood up.

Larios hooked his thumbs into the waist of his pants and stared at the pale, languid face. Even after seeing him, Larios found it hard to believe this young man could be wounded, that he could have fallen in battle. In the stillness, he suddenly felt the nearness of death—not so much thinking that it could happen to him but, rather, realizing how insignificant they both were. Their destiny was not in their hands but subject to some uncontrollable game of chance that had no respect or admiration for anyone. Finally he spoke, almost as if thinking out loud. "Where was he hit?"

Serafín lifted the blanket covering Valentín's chest.

"Here, below his shoulder, in the ribs. He lost a lot of blood, but he's not going to die."

"Damn," he murmured. "Did you take out the bullets?"

"Only the one in his thigh. The other was in too deep," Cipriano said, still looking at Valentín.

"He needs a doctor. I can send one. Or if you want, we could take him to Alamilla. It's still under my control."

"Don't even think about it," replied Cipriano.

Valentín Cobelo murmured a few scattered words, pieces of a dream. Julián moved closer. Cipriano and Serafín bent toward him.

"What do you want, muchacho?"

Trying to rise from the depths of unconsciousness, Valentín spoke. "Take me to the desert. I'm going to live. Don't let fear take over. Let's go, that's where we belong. We won, Cipriano. The important thing is we won."

"The desert it is, muchacho. Don't worry. Just leave it to us," he said, trying to contain his emotion and match the confidence in Valentín's voice.

"You heard him." Cipriano looked at Larios with satisfaction.

The visitor crouched down and spoke to Valentín. "It's Francisco Larios. I want to help. You know I have great respect for you. Perhaps you don't know this, but I consider myself your friend." He was silent, hoping for some kind of gesture, waiting for an answer that never came.

Larios straightened up and asked to speak with Cipriano alone.

"Look, here's the situation. I was after the gold too, but General Cobelo beat me to it. I was going to use it to buy weapons for the revolución."

"There's something you should know, General."

"Just a minute, don Cipriano, I haven't finished. A regiment of federales was sent on horseback to escort the train you just blew up. They're coming from Calamita. If they were all idiots, the revolution would be over by now. They'll arrive in Coauchapa tonight, and they won't be very happy when they learn their little train is not there."

Cipriano didn't need to hear any more. He fully understood the significance of this information, yet he chose to remain silent, hoping his silence would compel Larios to keep talking and offer a concrete proposition.

"I can distract the federales," continued Larios. "Give me half the gold, and I will make sure that Valentín Cobelo gets to the desert. I give you my word of honor."

Cipriano glanced toward the remains of the train, his eyes scanning the debris. Then he turned to survey the small flattened graves under the trees. "We lost more than eighty men taking that train. You have it easy, and you want half." He spoke without looking at Larios.

"I don't agree. This regiment of federales won't be easy to handle. Sooner or later, everything is won by bloodshed. That's my price."

Cipriano understood the subtle threat. "And if I refuse?"

"If you do not accept my offer, I'll have to fight you for the gold. My men are waiting over there. What I am asking is fair for what I offer. It is not in our best interest to fight each other. The rest of the federales could appear at any moment.

I'm not about to leave empty-handed. Remember Cipriano, we're in the middle of a revolution."

"If Valentín weren't injured, you wouldn't be in the same position."

"Perhaps not, but he is. And whether you believe it or not, I'm not happy about it."

Four of Cobelo's men went with General Larios, carrying three boxes of gold. Then they turned and followed their compañeros, who were already disappearing off in the distance.

They rode for more than five hours. The full moon had risen and shone brightly on them before they had gotten into the desert. The sky was a remote blackness. The few visible stars were scattered far apart; the rest were hiding. It was a lonely, empty night.

Valentín tried to open his eyes and emerge from the darkness that had swallowed him, but there was no light. He knew night had fallen, but he was far away and unable to bring himself back. He was alive. He repeated this over and over, somehow overcoming the loneliness that ached inside him. The soft rocking of the horses lulled him back into sleep.

Their muscles were masses of pain, and they were weary beyond human endurance. But the tension had been released, to be replaced by memories of their recent conquest and the full realization of what they had survived. Cobelo's men set up camp under the open sky. When they built their cooking fires, the dancing flames reminded them of their absent companions. They couldn't stand to look at one another; it only reminded them of the missing faces they would never see again. Some tried to forget their grief by cleaning a rifle or pistol, or by recounting their exploits in the attack, but they found no comfort. Even the trinkets they had liberated from the enemy seemed insignificant. Time stood still.

"Is he going to make it?" Julián asked Rarámuri, not doubting exactly, but seeking confirmation.

"He wants to. He's holding on, Julián. We have to wait for life to come back to him. Don't think about his dying. That will only attract death. You have to scare her off, make her feel unwelcome. Our general is strong and brave. I know how to heal him."

"I don't know what I'd do without him. I don't have anywhere to go, nothing to do. I've always wanted to be near him, to be like him. I worked on his ranch, like my parents. Once the patrón, Valentín's father, hit me with a horsewhip. I must have been about eleven. He was five or six years older, and he saw it. He was already tall, with his square jaw and sharp eyes. He didn't try to stop his father, he knew he couldn't, but I could tell by the way he looked at me that he was on my side. Then he started asking me to help him with things. He never talked much; you know how he is. He made me his horse wrangler, and ever since I've tried to do my best for him."

"In a little while, rub this leaf on his temples. Do both sides at the same time. Only do it once. I'll do it again later."

"Are you listening to me?"

"Yes, go ahead. I just wanted to show you what to do with this. I'm listening."

"After he burned the hacienda, he asked me if I wanted to go with him. I said sure, not knowing where to or what for. He gave me this gun. Look at the handle, all those engraved flowers. It's pure silver. I had already taught him how to use a knife. I learned that from my father. I never really understood why my general did so much for me. He even taught me to drink wine, although it still tastes strange to me."

"Ask him."

"No. Why should I? All my life he's made me feel like I mattered to him."

Rarámuri looked at him with affection. They shared a smile. "I'm going to sleep, Julián. Don't get scared if he screams. In his condition and with this medicine, he may see things we cannot even imagine. He's still fighting: with death and with himself."

NINE

EVERYBODY SAYS HE HELD UP A MILITARY TRAIN FULL OF GOLD and the government is looking for him. And not just them, but General Larios is looking for him too. They say Larios also wanted the gold. I heard he went south and let his men loose, that bunch of criminals. They also say, and I don't doubt it one bit, that as soon as he got that gold in his hands he ran off with all of it. Well, I heard he went back for that woman in Monreal and took her away with him. But who knows what really happened? They say she went crazy waiting for him—that she locked herself in her house and stands by her window every night until dawn waiting for him. Really, what terrible things go on! They say the train attack in Coauchapa was so brutal you could see the dead lined up from the Culebras River all the way into town and the river was red from all the blood. I heard he was shot lots of times, but the bullets just went right through him and he kept killing people right and left with his machete. He hates to use a gun. He's so cruel, he likes to see them suffer. May God keep him away from here; who knows what he'd do? Some people say he's dead, but I heard he stole some money from Francisco Larios and then ran into a train full of federales. Who can keep up with this revolution? So many new generals. I just don't know what to believe anymore. Over in Cocorita they swear he was killed and his men carried him off into the desert to bury him. They say the federales killed him when he tried to rob their train.

"Rosario, they're just rumors. Don't worry. If God wants him to come, he will. No one knows what God has planned, or how He is going to carry out His plan. Have some faith."
Cursed be the day he came into your life, hija.

Valentín's convalescence was marked by long, tedious days and nights. His arms lay by his sides, paralyzed and useless. His breath barely clung to him and his temperature matched that of the desert, burning and blistering by day, cold and shivering at night.

At times his face was like a pale mask of wax, at others a red-hot bronze bust. An indecipherable stillness surrounded him, full of intimate secrets, of peace without victory. To Cipriano and Rarámuri, Valentín's body was sacred, a mummified figure to be worshiped. But their desire to see beyond his injuries enabled them to perceive, while others could not, slight movements of his lips and throat, signs of a stifled scream unable to liberate itself. That unreleased cry was what filled them with hope.

"Remember, I asked you if you wanted to see what was in the unturned cards? You didn't want to because you thought you knew enough to calm your anguish and let you sleep. Now you're back. Always remember that behind what you know is something you don't know. I saw a lot of swords and I told you he was a dangerous man. The cards show he is sick but he'll be back, sure as my name is Castalia Leguado. And then you'll be sick, but there's no way to avoid it. That's just how it will be."

The days at La Higareda were long and empty. Resigned to waiting for their leader to come back from the black abyss that had swallowed him, the men made no decisions but allowed Cipriano and Serafin to think for them. Cobelo's men were imprisoned by this waiting; the walls surrounding them could be broken down only by their leader's voice, giving them an order—or by his death. His death would render them aimless, scattered without direction or purpose.

Those who had women held them close at night like frightened children. They would fall asleep without caressing them or satisfying their needs. It was enough just to have women close on these nights when even the blankets were steeped in isolation and uncertainty. The women understood the loneliness their men were suffering and knew they could not do much to alleviate it. They also knew that their duty to these men required them to remain strong so their men would have a soft bosom in which to rest their hopelessness. The women wanted the same things their men did, and more. They wanted their love to mean something and for their men to find shelter and warmth in their silence, wanted their smiles and commitment to endure until they and their men turned to dust, providing comfort and hope in the meantime. So they hid their tears. If a man were to let a tear escape in the darkness of night, his woman would offer her lips as a vessel so that his suffering would not be wasted, but would satisfy the thirst brought on by her extraordinary patience and compassion during General Cobelo's suffering.

"Poor men. We can be without them for long periods of time, but they cannot bear to be without one another. They are not that loyal to any woman."

"Ay, doña Celedonia," said one of the younger women, "they need us. Just look at the single ones. Those are the men you really feel sorry for."

"Sometimes I'd like to divide myself between them," added another one. "I mean in a good way. It hurts me to see them carry around so much grief. They look like beaten dogs."

The words of Castalia Leguado did little more than strengthen Rosario's resolve to remain at home, despite her mother's advice to go away. To leave would be to surrender, to give up on waiting. She didn't want to do that. Just to think that he would come back and find her gone made her shudder and worry even more than the waiting itself. Anxiety screamed at her from the mirror, from the bedsheets, from her hands, and demanded that she wait for him until she died.

When she entered Federico's study to attend to the matters he had left pending, she found respite and serenity. She was consoled by the memory of a man who never caused her a moment of worry because he had been blessed with a complete lack of passion. Theirs was a marriage that gently navigated the rivers of respect, tenderness, and routine. And it was there in the study that nightfall would find her drawing letters, completely absorbed in the intricate details of her lines.

Her work finished for the evening, she would get up from the desk knowing there was one day less to wait.

When supplies ran low, Serafín gathered the men and asked for five volunteers to go to Jalaplaca, the nearest town. No one spoke up. Serafín, smiling to himself, chose the men himself and sent them with Jerónimo Pastor.

"Why didn't you just pick them to start with?" asked Julián Vela.

"Just to see if anyone was itching to get out of here." He let out a caustic laugh. "Just to play with them a little."

In his delirium his father came to him, showing him the wounds the machetes had inflicted on his body. As he displayed each wound, his father would laugh grotesquely until finally he struck Valentín with a machete right between the eyes, cutting his face open from forehead to chin. The gash in his head opened wider and became a well, sucking his body into it. He fell, growing smaller and smaller, drowning in the agony of not being able to stop or even scream. His father kept laughing and watching him fall until Valentín could no longer see himself in the enfolding darkness. The image faded and gave way to a vast desert covered by a suffocating windstorm. Valentín rode his horse blindly, sweating from a heat more intense than any he had ever known, that emanated from the earth and had given birth to the storm. He knew it was day, but there was no sun. The ride was interminable, directionless and lonely, except at times when he was accompanied by a shadowy, faceless body.

Tearing at her soul, making a nest inside her, anguish came to Rosario. Valentín had forgotten her. She struggled in her bed each night, trying in vain to flee the nightmares that haunted her, leaving her breathless with despair and uncertainty. She cursed the day she first saw him and then cursed herself for not being able to wrench him from her memory, to erase the blazing image he had tattooed on her soul.

It was almost noon on the tenth day of waiting at La Higareda. Ceferino and three of his friends approached Serafín Machuca.

"Don't take this the wrong way," he said, "but we decided we want to leave and we want our part of the gold." He started out looking Serafín in the eye and finished staring at the ground, barely motioning to indicate the others with him.

Serafín listened to Ceferino without responding, drawing slowly on the cigarette he held between his teeth. He addressed the men standing beside Ceferino. "So what do you say? Or is he the only one who's going to speak? I want to hear from all of you."

"It's like Ceferino says. We're tired of running here and there and not really going anywhere," ventured one of the men. He stared at the ground and waited for one of the others to speak. None did.

"All right. If you want your gold, I'll give it to you. If you don't want to run around, as you say, that's fine. Come with me." He led them over to the opening in the rocks where they kept the gold.

Ceferino exchanged a timid smile of anticipation with the others. It had been much easier than they had imagined. Serafín understood their feelings.

Serafín invited them into the makeshift shelter. He was right behind them as they stood there stupefied, enraptured by what they saw.

"Stand over there. I'll give you your share in coins. It'll be easier to carry that way." Serafín grabbed bags of gold coins, much more than the four expected, and gave them to the men. Their hands were sweating and trembling. Mesmerized as they were by the sight of so much wealth, they didn't pocket the coins immediately.

"Put it away and go, quick now. And don't even think of telling anyone where we are."

"Of course not, Serafín. How could you think that?" Ceferino responded quickly. The four men turned and started for the door.

"Just one more thing."

All four turned back toward Serafín.

"Before you go I'm going to kill you."

By the tone of his voice, Ceferino and his friends knew that the only way they could hope to escape would be to defend themselves. They dropped the bags of gold and reached for their pistols. Before their hands touched their guns, they felt bullets entering their bodies, throwing them onto the bags they had planned to take with them.

"*Criatura,* my child, I've asked around and it really does seem that he's with his men. No one knows exactly where, but somewhere out in the desert. Believe me, Rosario, it's the truth. I heard that he and Larios divided up the gold from that military train, so you can be sure, when he comes for you, you won't go hungry."

"Thank you, doña Nicasia," said Rosario, smiling at her.

Cipriano and Rarámuri were surprised to see Valentín look at them. There was a sandy glint of satisfaction—triumph, even—in his eyes. His gaze was like a newly uncovered mirror.

"Don't try to say anything, Valentín. You're gonna be all right, you just wait, muchacho." Cipriano could barely contain his urge to scream for joy and hug his leader.

"I'm back, Cipriano."

"Don't push yourself, General. You still have some healing to do."

"How many men do we have?"

"About two hundred, maybe a few more. They're going to be so happy you're back with us."

"We lost a lot of men. What about her?"

Cipriano didn't know how to respond.

"I want to see her."

"Go to sleep and you'll see her. Later you can go see her. I'll even go with you to get her. Don't worry, muchacho. That woman is yours, like your own life."

"If I sleep I won't see her. I don't want ever to sleep again."

"Rest, General. It's been too much for you. Your soul has come back, but your body still needs sleep."

Cipriano asked Serafín for an explanation. "Why did you kill them?"

"Because they weren't loyal. Everybody else was willing to wait until the general recovered except them. That's why I killed them, at least that's the main reason. I wasn't happy to do it; don't think I did it to be mean. You should have seen their faces when they saw the gold. I knew when they got to town they'd go crazy with so much money; they would have talked."

Valentín Cobelo woke up as the darkness was losing its battle with the dawn. Cipriano watched him in silence. Valentín dressed himself and went out into the desert. He felt a slight throbbing in his ribs, but it was tolerable. He walked into the early sunlight, passing out of Cipriano's view. The men were still sleeping. It was cold.

He needed to feel the earth, dig his boots deep in the dirt. The desert opened to him as he walked. The distant mountains appeared through the early morning haze, and although he was walking in the opposite direction, he felt each step was bringing him closer to Rosario Alomar.

Valentín grew light-headed and his feet became heavy. It was difficult to lift them off the ground. He felt himself spinning, and the desert reeled dizzyingly. He was a child sitting on a merry-go-round horse, smiling at his mother. Each time he passed they waved at each other. The horse kept going up and down. Then his mother was gone, and so were all the other children. He looked desperately for someone he knew, but there was no one. Gripped by fear, Valentín pleaded for someone to stop the machine, but his screams only echoed in the empty space as the carousel spun faster and faster through an ethereal landscape. Guided by instinct, he jumped from the spinning merry-go-round and crashed to the ground. He rolled and lay still, unconscious, not knowing how long he lay there. The sun was bright when he opened his eyes, and it blinded him for an instant. Lying still, he felt the earth with his hands, felt his cheek on the hard ground.

Where am I going? It feels good here on the ground. I'm thirsty. Rosario, I want you. I want you here, pressed against my body, the two of us melting together until we disappear completely. We'll become sand and take off with the wind, Rosario.

He managed to stand and, haltingly, begin to retrace his steps. Cipriano and Rarámuri found him. He greedily drank the water they offered him. They had brought his horse and helped him mount.

As they drew closer to La Higareda, the men gradually became aware of his presence. There he was, General Valentín Cobelo, on his horse. Even in broad daylight the image seemed surreal. With the sun behind him, he looked like a desert warrior. His men had to squint against the sun. A strange feeling passed through them, carrying a trace of fear with it. Behind Valentín were Cipriano and Rarámuri. Perhaps it was their presence that brought them all out of their trance. The first to yell and throw his hat in the air was Julián Vela.

"Viva mi general Valentín Cobelo!"

Valentín made a valiant effort not to faint, his pride now stronger than his body.

The men surrounded him, shouting and firing into the air. It was as if a spell had been broken, a curse lifted. Some of them jumped on their horses and spurred them to rear up. They took out their machetes and waved them in the air, pretending to fight. The women smiled and watched their men celebrate. Sweating, exhausted, Valentín Cobelo smiled too, happy to be the leader of men so eager to follow him, even to their deaths.

"Cipriano, distribute the gold."

The cries grew even louder, bullets flew, machetes flashed in the air. Valentín dismounted and walked toward his cabin. He dropped onto his bed. Cipriano, who had followed him silently, grew worried, joy disappearing from his face.

"Don't worry. I'm all right. I'm just tired. I'll be stronger tomorrow. What? You think after all that celebrating I'd let myself die? Come on, go divide up the gold. We're moving out tomorrow."

TEN

IT WAS EVENING WHEN VALENTIN COBELO RODE INTO MON-
real, guarded by Cipriano and Rarámuri. Julián Vela, Serafín
Machuca, and nearly a hundred *macheteros* followed behind.
The townspeople regarded them with shock and dismay,
which was quickly replaced by fear as they ran to seek refuge
in their homes, already feeling the vertigo brought on by the
threat of renewed violence in their peaceful hamlet. They
bolted doors, drew curtains, shuttered windows, and whispered quietly to one another. A few dared to peek out at the
revolutionaries. Only the sound of the horses' hooves on the
paved street could be heard. Fear and uncertainty filtered
slowly through walls and souls.

Accustomed to the routine of daily life in Monreal, languid
afternoons that faded into serene evenings, Rosario Alomar

perceived the sudden quiet as an omen. She lifted her pen from the land deed she was working on and focused her attention on the silence, pouring in from outside like a sweet scent. *It's him! Those far-off sounds belong to Valentín Cobelo and his men and their horses!*

Doña Severina came to the study door in hopes that her daughter would appease her fears, tell her it wasn't true—*Just stay calm; it is other men, on some other mission*—hoping that evening would gently replace afternoon and that night would tiptoe in through the windows as it always did and they would go to bed and try to sleep, still waiting.

"He's come, Mamá."

Doña Severina ran to her daughter. She ached to tell her to stay, that she was not the woman for that kind of man, for only God knows what kind of life, yet all she could manage was a hug, a gesture of farewell that had begun long ago.

As she felt her mother's arms around her, Rosario tried to imagine what was about to happen. During her long wait she had decided precisely how she would act and what she would say when this moment arrived. Now it was upon her and none of that mattered anymore. All she could do was take a chance, bet everything on impulse.

She heard the horses drawing nearer, in cadence, rhythmic, not rushing the inevitable. Valentín knew that he would soon see Rosario and that she would come away with him.

Rosario pulled away from her mother's embrace and lied to her. "I won't leave you, Mamá."

"You and I both know that you will. He's coming for you. You've been waiting for him, calling him. You would never forgive me or yourself if you stayed."

Valentín and his men stopped in front of don Celestino

Alomar's house. Valentín dismounted and walked to the door. As he knocked a pang of fear passed through him like a meteor.

Rosario opened the door. She had not been wrong. He had been responsible for the silence that had taken hold of her soul. Her initial surprise was replaced by the certainty that her wait was over. As he stood before her, Rosario knew that Valentín Cobelo had blocked the path of the worm of bitterness within her. He opened the door to all that was unpredictable, liberating her from the struggle to find a meaningful life, to experience love.

He smiled to himself, as if with his smile he could speak every word of joy and pleasure he knew and never before dared utter, because until now he had never understood what they meant. There she was, waiting for him, loving him, wanting him as much as he had been desiring her. She had lit the fire of passion inside him and fed it with the thorny branches of absence and distance. Bathed in the heat of those flames, Rosario waited for him to speak.

"I have come for you. I don't want to force you. I can't promise anything. I am all that I have and you are all that I want."

Without waiting for her answer, he kissed her. Her lips opened like windows to her soul, so that Valentín could enter. They explored each other as if the two of them were no longer part of this world but lost in a drunken rapture. Each kiss was more intense, a new manifestation of the infinite number of kisses he had tenderly saved for her. All impatience, despair, and anguish was erased because time no longer existed, had never existed. Not one instant had passed since she first saw him. She wanted to speak of love, but to do so would have meant interrupting her long-awaited pleasure, and she felt the word was not enough to express the emotion that possessed her.

Rosario's lips were too much for Valentín. She made him burn with passion, made him delirious, aroused him. He felt as though his soul might escape, so he pulled away to look at her again. Out of breath and exhilarated, she gazed back at him without saying a word. Both were shaken by bliss. Valentín called for the mare he had brought and placed it in front of her. Rosario turned to her mother and found herself unable to beg forgiveness for the overpowering need to leave with this man who was her destiny.

Doña Severina watched her daughter get on the horse and gallop fearlessly away toward the desert. Alone with the swirling dust, she went back into the house, weeping, to await the comfort of night.

The wild race against time and distance continued deep into the desert. Valentín and the woman next to him led the charge, spurring and whipping their mounts. The wind was a wall trying to impede them, but it was no match for the intensity of their assault. As they penetrated farther into the desert the wind grew stronger, angered at its own impotence, and the sun disappeared. Surprised by the strong, arrogant presence at Valentín Cobelo's side, the sun drew the night closer, becoming one with it, enfolding the two riders and swallowing them. They moved across this infinite space, part of a slumbering god's dream where the stars were clear springs in a naked sky.

The heavy darkness clung to Rosario, making it impossible for her to see the mare she was riding. Listening to the rhythmic hoofbeats of the horses and feeling Valentín Cobelo's solid presence, she surrendered herself completely to a newly discovered freedom. So firm in her decision to continue forward was she that the wind moved aside to let her pass. She was drawn into the sensual, frenzied gallop, anxious to reach an unknown place where she and Valentín could embrace once again, free from constraints, doubts, and certainties.

Excited by the ecstasy he sensed and by the blind loyalty of the mare matching his gait, Valentín's stallion flew with Rosario's mare through the desert to a solitary and barren land where their neighs, their manes, their passion would erupt in an endless frenzied dance of love.

Rosario ceased being flesh, dreams, thoughts and was reborn as pleasure, emotion, voluptuousness. Nothing existed before this moment. Nothing else held any significance for her. She was removed from the world; it was no longer of importance to her. Nor was it to Valentín Cobelo, who felt her presence inside him, joining his soul and expanding to include the stars that guided them to the bed he had seen only in his imagination and that now seemed inadequate before their vast nakedness, their endless skin, their fevered hands incapable of resting or being still. The wind raged and howled, furious at being locked away from their passion, until it finally gave up and wandered off. Valentín and Rosario immersed themselves in the uncontainable, unstoppable, distanceless pleasure, deliriously believing their union complete only if they could plant themselves in one another, their roots entwined, woven into depths of desire far beyond this tiny desert. After the interminable waiting, the melting insomnia that had punished Rosario in that other time and place, they were torches of yearning, the past now erased by the sands of the desert, lost in the darkness, cleansed from her soul.

They were oblivious to the sun beating on the roof of their shelter, trying to set it ablaze, looking for cracks in the window frames, holes in the walls, and finally locking itself in with them. The lovers' bodies gave off a heat more intense and asphyxiating than any sun. They drank each other's sweat only to burn again with passion, as they searched for and found each other in that oven of skin and caresses.

"Cipriano, I think the earth has eaten them."

"It swallowed them, Julián, that's what it did."

The next day Rosario and Valentín rode alone. "Take strength from the earth," he said. He showed it to her as his domain, his secret, while she burned under a sun that was suffocating her, like the need that compelled them to stop and lie down in that ocher desert. Valentín tore at her, covering her belly, her nipples, her thighs, her cheeks, her arms with burning earth until she became earth and he buried his hands, his anxiety, his manhood.

During those days and nights of impatience and uncertainty, the men and women at La Higareda kept busy, though the passion was not theirs and they were overwhelmed by heat. The sun haunted them with its lacerating stillness. They felt it cutting into their backs, their heads, their faces, their arms. They could not flee its harshness. And still General Cobelo's door remained closed, guarding the untransferable, inexplicable, sacred secret within.

They asked no questions, they didn't even talk. They waited. They didn't see the door open at dawn, but they heard the horses head out into the desert, toward the splendor of a new day challenging the darkness, eager to display its full glory.

When Valentín and Rosario returned later in the morning, the others bowed their heads, not daring to look. Only when the door closed again did they look up, imagining.

"Will we ever go back out in the world, Valentín?"

"There is no other world for us, Rosario. We owe ourselves to this desert, which brought us together."

"Sometimes I feel I'm being consumed."

"Be careful what you say. Words have a power of their own."

"Hold me, Valentín. Don't ever leave me."

As he embraced her he witnessed the birth of loneliness between them. To banish it he promised himself, *I'll never again be without you, not even in death.* The battering wind ripped his thoughts from his soul and scattered them in the surrounding desert and beyond as a warning, a threat. He kissed her on the lips, sealing a promise Rosario never heard.

That night she heard the voices in the desert for the first time. They called to her, scratching at the door and the windows, crying desperately, magnifying the silence of this dark, lost place. She thought about her mother. She could feel the loneliness torturing her mother, but she was unable to cry. The wind whipped at the walls. She pressed against Valentín, taking refuge from her fears, desperately needing to feel him close to make them go away. She was suddenly struck by the brutal realization that she could touch him without desiring him. She could sleep peacefully next to him. She had grown accustomed to his presence.

ELEVEN

ROSARIO AWAKENED WELL PAST NOON, QUIETLY EXCITED, AND lay in bed with her eyes open. She knew she was far from everything familiar to her. She looked at the austere walls surrounding her for the first time.

An older woman in a white blouse and dark skirt came into the room, carrying two plates of food. Rosario sat up as she approached.

"You're awake now, señora? I brought you something to eat."

Her voice was caring. Rosario was grateful that it was a woman who spoke to her. It seemed such a long time since she had talked to another woman.

"What's your name?"

"Adelaida Morones, at your service. Go ahead, eat."

"Could you open a window, please? I need some light. What is this?"

"Snake meat with broth. It's delicious. I'll bring you some tortillas."

"No, it's fine like this. Don't go."

"I'll get you some water and be right back. Don't worry, the general will be back soon."

"Valentín?" asked Rosario, just to pronounce his name, to confirm that she was with him, to regain a sense of reality in this new world she was just discovering.

"Ay, señora, who else? Eat. I'll get your water. Nobody will bother you here." Adelaida Morones left, closing the door behind her. Rosario began to eat, slowly at first, then with greater appetite. She had not eaten snake meat since her father left. Its sweet taste and tenderness reminded her of him. He liked hunting snakes; he would skin and cook them himself. Then she thought about her mother, and anxiety, like a root forcing its way through rocks, pushed its way into her thoughts. She wanted to run to her, to escape. Nervously, impulsively, she stood up, throwing the plates on the floor, and ran to the door. She opened it, wanting to scream, but stopped and looked at faces she had never seen before, men, Indian women, dark, young, old, and horses, herbs, cactus, all enveloped in the sun's yellow haze.

They looked at Rosario through silent eyes set in stoic faces. She felt their stares and her skin flushed with modesty, shamed to realize that they must have been staring at her like this from the moment she arrived. Her secret, her intimacy with Valentín, was somehow known to these strange, unknown people. Smiling to calm herself, she closed the door.

As she lay down again, she wasn't sure whether she wanted to see Valentín again or not. *I don't really know anything about him, and he knows less about me.*

Adelaida Morones interrupted her thoughts by bringing Rosario a pitcher of water. Adelaida saw the plates on the floor but pretended not to. "Here's some fresh water. Drink it. I don't know how Rarámuri always manages to find water in the middle of the desert. Seems like some kind of witchcraft to me."

Rosario smiled. She liked this woman. For a moment, as she sipped the water, she asked herself what a woman like this was doing in such a place.

"Who is Rarámuri?"

"Oh, he takes care of the general. He's a Tarahumara Indian. His real name is Baltasar Juan. He's a good man, you'll see. Do you need anything else? If you want I can come back later."

"Don't go. Tell me, doña Adelaida—"

"Just call me Adelaida."

"Adelaida. What do the women do around here?"

"The same as anywhere, señora. When the men are here we take care of them, when they're not we wait for them, but there are always a few around."

"Why did you come to live here?"

"Because that's what the general wanted. His men live here, and so do the women who follow them. Out here the general makes the rules, we follow them."

"And you, Adelaida, forgive me, but—"

"Don't worry about it. Yes, I'm old, must be about fifty or so. I don't really know for sure. I followed the general when he and some of the others at the hacienda decided to leave. Julián Vela is my nephew; he's more like a son, though. My own children are all dead. So I stayed with Julián, but I also wanted to follow the general. I've known him since he was just a boy."

"What hacienda?"

"The general's. You should have seen it. It was so beautiful."

"What happened to it?"

"Ay, niña, you better ask him yourself. Forgive me, but I'm only here to serve him, nothing more. You should talk with him if you have questions."

"Valentín Cobelo is not my master."

Adelaida Morones did not respond. She simply turned and left the room.

Rosario sat on the bed, thinking how she was far from everything, how she had been living for days in an altered state, a kind of vertigo. *I abandoned myself.*

She went out again and walked among men and women. They stopped all activity as she passed, stood up, and took off their hats. The women smiled shyly. The earth was scalding and the iron sun burned down on this tiny village, not much more than a mirage. Nearby some horses lingered, not fenced or tied. A few of the women managed a timid greeting, but the men remained silent and, as soon as she had passed, went back to sharpening their machetes, cleaning their rifles, weaving hats. One man was playing a guitar. He stopped. "Continue," Rosario said graciously. He went back to his song, looking down at the strings. *"He rode through the hills and the mountains took pity on him. He searched and searched until he found her and she gave up her cold passion. They were hard times, days of revolution, but he had no cause other than her eyes, her love. . . ."*

She came upon Julián Vela and recognized him immediately. He was the man who had brought her Federico's body. She wanted to say something because he was a link to her past. No words came to her, and so he spoke.

"We are here to serve you, señora, always."

Rosario nodded her head slightly to acknowledge his words, then turned around, retracing her steps. When she reached the women making tortillas she sat down with them. Surprised, the women stopped and looked at her. Without a word she began kneading the *masa*. The women smiled and resumed their work.

Foreign, a stranger, bubbling over with eagerness yet unsure of her place in this new world, Rosario patted out tortillas. It reminded her of home and a similar monotony, but in a world that was her own, in which she felt safe, where she belonged. She reminded herself that she had always made her own choices and would continue to do so. No one was going to tell her what to do.

"There don't seem to be enough women for all these men," she said, without looking up, in an attempt to initiate womanly conversation. They giggled.

"Not all of them want a woman around. Most of them don't; then they walk around lonely, not knowing what to do," said one young woman, causing new laughter. "The general doesn't like having too many women around either."

These were young women, with plain oval faces. Some were tall. Their breasts moved rhythmically with their patting of tortillas. Despite the intense heat, they barely perspired.

"Do you like the desert?"

"This is where the men make their home."

"But aren't you bored?"

They looked at one another, not sure what she meant. No one answered.

"Were all of you at the hacienda?"

"No, only those two," said a woman, pointing at two others who were shucking corn a few feet away, "and Adelaida."

"Do you like living here?"

"Ay, señora, it's where we live."

She could not stand the sun beating down on her head one more instant, making her sweat. She stood up.

"Thank you for helping us, señora."

Rosario waved her hand and returned to the house.

Her eyes surveyed the walls, arid, empty. They are the walls of the desert, of these women, she thought. The rough wooden table, the four harsh chairs. No paintings or portraits, no rugs, no flowers. With the door closed, no sound entered in. Sitting there she realized that the desert is silence, solitude.

The world could disappear, all civilization could be destroyed, and I could sit here and never know it.

She walked across the room, stepping on a pale scorpion. She placed her hands on the table, not knowing what to do with them. *I have nothing, only Valentín. What happens now?*

Wanting to see herself in the mirror and thinking she might have missed it earlier, Rosario looked around the room. There was none. She rushed up the stairs to the loft and stopped when she saw the nearly empty space. She walked toward an old armoire as if it were a window with a fresh view of something, of Monreal maybe. Opening it, she saw another wall, two pairs of pants, three shirts, a leather jacket: Valentín's clothes. She leaned against it and looked around her. Still no mirror. Agitated by not being able to look at herself, she felt as if she were choking. *I'm going to forget what I look like. I didn't come here to die.*

She repeated those words to herself, unable to think clearly, to understand her feelings, unable to find anything that could explain this uninhabited world she had become part of, this world that tried to absorb her. *No! It's not mine. I don't want it to be mine!*

She slowly descended the stairs, her heart racing. Obsessed with finding a mirror, Rosario went to the door.

"Adelaida! Adelaida!"

A few moments later, Adelaida appeared.

"I would like to take a bath," she said, without having thought of it until she spoke. "Please bring me a mirror."

"Sí, señora, right away."

Rosario closed the door and looked at her clothes. They were the same ones she wore the day Valentín had come for her. She was overtaken with pangs of desire for him. *I need him. No, not anymore. It cannot be.* She almost spoke the words out loud.

She had to take charge of her own body.

Adelaida Morones came in with two other women, carrying a large metal tub.

"Here's the mirror." Adelaida gave her a square engraved-silver mirror. "We'll just fill the tub, señora."

Taking a few steps away, Rosario looked at herself in the mirror. Her face was clean. She wet her chapped lips with her tongue. She looked into her eyes, searching, until her image became blurred by hesitant tears. *I feel so alone.* She wiped her eyes. *You are Rosario Alomar.* Far away, like a drop of water falling in her memory, she heard her father call her Rosarito.

"The water is ready, señora."

She turned toward the women, smiled pleasantly, and closed her soul. They helped her undress.

Over and over she cupped her hands and splashed her face. Adelaida poured water on her back from a bowl. The water caressed her, cleansing her as she regained awareness of her body. She had forgotten it completely and was now joyfully rediscovering it. Rosario rubbed herself gently, then lowered her head and let the water pour over her hair.

She raised her head again and saw Valentín framed in the doorway, sunlight streaming all around him. Modestly she covered her breasts. He gazed at her. Adelaida left quickly.

Rosario looked at Valentín standing in the doorway and let her arms drop. He walked slowly toward her as she stood up, never taking her eyes off him. Entranced, Valentín's eyes were frozen on her body. He didn't want to hurry, but Rosario's eyes were like a magnet, pulling him closer.

"Valentín," she said firmly, her hair dripping and water running down her neck, her shoulders, her proud breasts, "I am yours."

When she woke up, Valentín Cobelo was looking at her. Rosario tried to sit up, but he gestured for her not to.

"I was outside with the women. Everything was so strange. They have no lives of their own, no hopes or dreams. I don't think they ever expect to."

Valentín didn't respond. He kept looking at her, displaying no emotion.

"I don't want to become part of the desert. Let's get away from here."

"The desert is in my blood."

"It's dead. It's brilliant, but it's a corpse."

"I can't, Rosario. I *am* the desert."

A silence descended between them. It was an impossible situation. With her head on his chest, Rosario withdrew deep into herself, walking in fear in a place where the seeds of regret had already sprouted.

Days of nothing but sun, helpless, exhausting, interminable. Trapped in a prison. The world was far away, unreachable. She rode out to the desert just to get a breath, to feel the vastness of that arid land. Severina was a shadow, a distant memory. Freezing nights with howling winds, trapped by the falling darkness, an impenetrable wall. Days and nights with no respite. Silence. Cipriano's kindness was a window allowing her to see into the distance. Yes, sometimes Valentín was tender and looked at her with love as he sipped his wine and smoked his cigar. Time passed as if it didn't even exist. Rosario waited.

"Here, in the desert, is where Valentín became a man," Cipriano told her one day. He walked slowly, so the importance of his words would not be lost. "This is where he found solace. If you can't accept him the way he is, then leave him. You should know that he will never leave you. You shouldn't have come into his life, but that's fate. It dealt you a bad hand, señora."

"Your words frighten me."

"I'm only telling you what you already know. Women always know."

Rosario pretended to understand the silence, and at first she liked greeting dawn on horseback with Valentín at her side. The days began to wear on her and words, tired of waiting, spilled out.

"Tell me about yourself, Valentín."

"I am what you see."

"Tell me about your past, what you want out of life."

"I don't want anything. My past doesn't matter, as yours

doesn't matter. The only thing that matters is that we are together."

"Don't you understand me?"

"Yes, I understand you, Rosario. But I can't do anything. My life has already been chosen, and I've brought you into it."

"You don't care what I want, what I feel. I don't want this hell! All that I have to live for is needing your body! Some day I'm going to leave if you don't take me away from here."

"You can't leave, because I won't let you go."

Rosario wanted to love him, but she felt defeated and afraid.

That night she said no to him for the first time. She stayed awake waiting for him to fall asleep, for the wind to come. When it tore at the walls she decided to confront it, to overcome the fear that it caused in her, to draw strength from the voices constantly calling her. She went outside. Engulfed by the overwhelming darkness, she started walking. The wind clawed at her, its cries raking her skin. Rosario endured the harsh wind on her face and the arrogance and stubbornness of the night, which refused to welcome her. Barefoot, she offered her naked feet to the hard, invisible ground. As her fear mounted, her determination grew along with it. Memories of her dead husband and father took hold of her and she called out to them, unable to distinguish their voices amid the screams and moans that called and reached out to her.

"Come back, Rosario." Valentín took her by the arm, and she felt herself fall into a deep hole, toward a distant, barely perceptible light, remembered from some vague dream. The light came from Valentín's eyes. She felt herself being carried.

She begged, "Take me away from here, Valentín. If we don't leave, I'll die."

"Then we'll die together, Rosario," Valentín responded softly, in a sad voice she had never heard.

Late that afternoon, Rosario awoke. Valentín had stayed with her, wiping the sweat from her forehead, calming her when the nightmares made her call out the names of her mother, father, and the man at her side. Barely awake, she drank a tea that Rarámuri had prepared for her.

"Yesterday I thought I had died, that I had become a tortured soul wandering about in the wind."

"The desert plays tricks on you." Valentín's words were imbued with sweetness.

Rosario caressed his face and his hair. *I'm not going to love you, Valentín. If I love you I'll go crazy,* she thought, as she kissed his lips.

"You are his other half, señora, the part he was missing. That's why he can never let you go. I've already told him so. Even if he wanted to, it's beyond him. And he means something to you, I don't know just what yet, but I know it's something; that's why you are here. It's true, his need is stronger."

"It's not love, Cipriano. All I can think of is death. I could love him, but I don't want to. If I do, I'll be lost forever. He doesn't love me either."

"Who knows what love really is? Believe me, no one knows." Cipriano smiled sadly. "Sometimes it's nice to think of consolation, passion, or even fear as love."

"Cipriano, help me escape. Please, I beg you!"

"Don't ask that of me. I understand how you feel, but

there are things you don't understand. I don't know what to call them. I just know they come from inside, from the soul. Look at these veins." Cipriano showed her his muscular arms, covered with thick, raised veins. "Pick one, two, as many as you want. What I feel for that boy is running through all of them."

"Swear to me that you won't tell him what I've told you, what I asked you to do."

"I promise. But it doesn't change anything, doña Rosario, not a thing."

So Rosario waited, and the day came when Valentín had to go do what the other part of his life required of him. She begged him to take her with him, not to leave her. But he told her he couldn't and left with his men, telling Jerónimo Pastor to take care of her. After two days she tied a couple of canteens under her skirts and told Jerónimo she was going out riding, but she wasn't crazy enough to try and escape because she knew she'd get lost. She rode farther and farther from La Higareda, sure she could tame the desert and find her way back to life, convinced that only her passion had died.

TWELVE

WHEN HE RETURNED, VALENTIN WANTED TO KILL JERONIMO, but Cipriano stopped him.

"You let her go because you didn't dare change, muchacho. You know the truth. Go ahead and kill him if you want."

Valentín didn't kill him, but instead told him to go away, to leave forever. Jerónimo Pastor no longer existed in Valentín's eyes. He had become the image of the day that Rosario Alomar had run off.

He waited for night to come and rode out into it so the voices of the desert could tell him where to find her. Those voices suffered along with him because they had been unable to stop her. They ran and flew through the desert with him, desperate, victims of deceit.

I swear I will find you, Rosario. And if I have to kill you to never lose you again, I will; then I'll kill myself. I will leave no stone unturned, no body of water uncrossed until I find you. I will destroy your hiding place. I will kill anyone who hides you from me. I will spill so much blood that it will cover the desert. I will tear open every grave I find to make sure you are not hiding there from me, Rosario, I promise.

They say that Valentín Cobelo gathered up all his men and left the desert. Some people say he divided them up in teams of twenty and made them spread out, looking for Rosario Alomar. I heard that her mother was still in Monreal, waiting, not knowing where her daughter was.

His men didn't ask any questions. They couldn't understand his obsession, but they obeyed. No longer restrained, they were happy to be active again, eager to look for her until they found her and brought her back alive.

"Julián, take six men with you and go to Monreal. She will go back there someday. Make sure her mother doesn't go anywhere. If you find her, send me word, then bring her back. Make her swallow the desert, let the sun burn and tear her apart. I want her to know that when she enters the desert she's with me again."

And so the search for Rosario Alomar began. Their horses ripped into the earth and their machetes showed up in so many places that there was no way of knowing how many they were. No one could count the dismembered, disfigured bodies left behind by those merciless men. The entire hunt was a bloodbath. They burned everything, leaving behind only rising smoke.

Rosario left no trace, nor did she go home to her mother. She just kept running. She knew if she stopped, Valentín would find her.

Opalina, Ciencasa, Maintilla, Riovado, Ojarito, and only God knows how many other pueblos succumbed to the fire and rage of Valentín Cobelo's blinding pain. A woman that matched Rosario Alomar's description had been in some of the houses, a woman they had seen before, but they had heard of her beauty and how she had fled from the desert, running from a man called Valentín Cobelo, whom they had never seen either. They thought he was just another legend, until a duststorm brought him in, riding wildly because he knew she had been there. But had it really been her? He tore through the pueblo anyway, without mercy.

Rosario, in her lonely, incessant travels, heard the stories about the murderer searching for a woman who had cast a spell on him. Once she attended a wedding where the entire town prayed for God to keep the assassin away. In every house there was a vessel of holy water and the scissors were left open for protection from evil, so that if the woman came around, she would leave immediately without casting a spell on them as she had in other places.

What did I do to you, Valentín? What have you done to yourself? We're destroying everything and everyone. I'm fading away as I try to escape your fury. I can't see my mother, and you're in agony, consuming yourself with despair. My strength is gone. Maybe the time has come for us to accept defeat. Can't we just forget? How did we ever become one?

Basilia Liu watched over him and tended to his needs, feeling the anguish eating away at him, not letting him speak, making him sit for hours drinking wine slowly, drop by drop, as if it were his own blood. No woman could satisfy him. When Basilia's cards said he should be calm, that he would have her again, his anguish only increased. His impatience was more painful than the uncertainty. Then he left, eager to catch up with the fate Basilia's cards had foretold. But he couldn't find her.

They say that Basilia offered to break her vow of never sleeping with anyone again and that Valentín refused her because he could not conceive of being with any woman other than Rosario Alomar. And they say that Basilia Liu closed her business and moved south with some of her girls, letting go of old memories she no longer wanted.

To think that there were days, weeks even, when sleeplessness haunted me as I waited for you. We will meet again, Valentín. I'm tired of running from you. I don't have you anymore, I barely have myself. There is nothing left to live for. Very little remains of what I once had. How I long to go back to the days when I waited eagerly for you, when I dreamed only of seeing you, clinging to the hope of your return. What I imagined was nothing like what actually happened. I only imagined love, Valentín.

Later that night, Rosario awakened suddenly from a nightmare of desiring Valentín again. Sweating as she had in the desert, she felt his burning hands on her body. Burying herself in the sheets, she bit them and swallowed her desire so he would not devour her again.

They made doña Severina swear on her knees that she didn't know where her daughter was. She could only tell them that she had received a letter, assuring her that she would be home soon. So Julián Vela stayed on guard, waiting for Rosario to fulfill her promise.

They came through here in groups of twenty, as they did in other places, ragged and disheartened, their horses lean and broken. Some people thought they had been defeated by the *constitucionalistas* or Pancho Villa's men or President Huerta's army, but no, Valentín Cobelo's loyal machete-wielding soldiers only suffered from exhaustion and hunger. They say that some of them, tired of all the killing, would beg for food in villages, and someone always showed mercy on those poor men, who had lost contact with their general and were drifting, searching for that treacherous woman. They were far from their desert home and hoped only for an army to take them in or for some place to rest. If any of them mentioned Rosario Alomar's name the townspeople would cross themselves and turn their backs, horrified to have proof of the infamous legend. Was it a true story? But we did see them, those poor stragglers.

Stop the killing, Valentín. I can't go on without seeing my mother. I'm tired. I've had so many names I can hardly remember my real one. Time melts away in this solitude, holding me prisoner. Sometimes I just wish you'd find me and put an end to this insane life we've created. It's destroying us both.

General Francisco Larios received orders from a higher command to take care of Valentín Cobelo. "He's not even a true revolucionario, yet he has sown much destruction and for no clear reason." He was ordered to find Valentín and kill him. Larios did not think it was fair to mount an all-out attack without warning him first. He thought it unseemly, given that he had a personal relationship with General Cobelo, so he sent his troops to find him, then spoke directly with him.

"They've ordered me to kill you. I don't know if I am able, but I will try. I just wanted you to know because I respect you."

"I'm involved with another matter at the moment, but if this is what you want, then so be it. I only want to ask your word that if you defeat me you won't lock up my men or shoot them. Just let them go. Don't humiliate them."

"I give you my word and ask yours in return. How many men do you have?"

"About two hundred."

"It's going to be hard for you, General Cobelo. I've got more than that."

"We've talked enough. Thank you for your graciousness, General Larios. We'll see each other again soon."

Valentín Cobelo's two hundred macheteros and General Francisco Larios's six hundred revolucionarios met on the open plain at Trescaminos.

Ever cautious, Serafín Machuca had been clever enough to bring along the machine gun he had liberated during the military train incident.

"With this we can't lose, *mi general*. We may all die, but we'll take them down with us."

"Still looking for death, muchacho?"

"What did you expect me to do, give up? I'm already dead, Cipriano."

"How long are you going to fight?"

"Until we win. This is my final battle."

"And then what? You can't just give in, Valentín."

"If that's how you see it, then that's how it is."

"You gave her the chance to leave. If you had really wanted it, she'd be with you now."

"For once I let myself hope. I thought she would stay."

"You expected too much of her."

"I love her, Cipriano. I swear to God I love her."

"You should have realized it sooner."

"You talk a lot of nonsense."

Cipriano let out a loud chuckle.

"What are you laughing at?"

"Nothing. You should always laugh before going in to battle."

At some distance, like a narrow wavy belt, Francisco Larios's troops appeared on the horizon, walking into the sun, which was just beginning to appear, an impartial witness.

There was not a hill or even a rock in sight. Three roads met on the wide plain, then went off in separate directions.

Serafin was buried up to his waist in hot sand, the machine gun next to him at eye level. He had gripped the instrument's handle from the first moment he had lowered himself into the hole. Behind him, on horseback, almost three hundred yards away, the rest of Valentín Cobelo's men formed a long line, silent, still.

Federico Larios's men formed several groups and watched confidently.

There are a lot of them. They could come at us one group at a time. If we can't hold out, my men are finished and this whole thing is damned. Larios, you and your causes, your loyalties.

You're going to lose because you didn't want to fight, and because fate already smiled on you once. You've lost, Larios, because you know you might lose, thought Valentín, as he observed the formation of the distant riders.

"He'll become impatient, muchacho."

"Ay, he's got a lot of men."

"And fear. You know he's afraid."

"He's lined them up in groups. We'll make a semicircle around Serafín, and when they come at us we'll open up. We'll just have to wait for them."

General Francisco Larios sent the men on horseback out to the flanks at full gallop, a position from which they couldn't possibly see Serafín Machuca, half buried in the sand. Valentín's men held tight during the oncoming charge, forcing their opponents closer until Serafín had them in range. He opened fire on them and Larios's men fell, buried under their dying horses.

Before Cobelo's men could regroup, Larios sent two more groups, wider than before. Swinging his weapon wildly from side to side, Serafín missed some of the revolucionarios, and they got near enough to engage in close combat with the cobelistas. Then Larios sent in two more contingents and Serafín focused on them, trying to kill all of them to make up for the ones he had missed. At such close range, Valentín Cobelo's men were much more adept than the attackers.

Valentín reestablished the semicircle around Serafín Machuca and waited.

Francisco Larios spread out his men to attack the cobelistas head on. Valentín recognized the new strategy and ordered his men to attack from the sides, while Serafín, pivoting from the waist, held the rest at bay. Larios smiled in satisfaction at Cobelo's move and ordered a full attack. As the revolucionarios drew nearer, the cobelistas stopped and began to retreat, followed closely by Larios's men, who soon met up with Serafin and his machine gun.

"Come closer, you bastards, come on!" screamed Serafin, shooting wildly.

Larios quickly realized that he had fallen into a trap. Only a few of his men would escape the machine gun to enter into direct contact with the enemy.

Valentín commanded his men to turn around and confront those revolucionarios who had managed to escape Serafin Machuca's gunfire. Unsure, afraid, trapped, Francisco Larios's men didn't know whether to stand and fight or retreat, so they kept on shooting, overwhelmed by the thought that every time they missed a target their own deaths drew nearer.

Larios sought out the man wielding the machine and galloped toward him, shooting. When Serafin felt he was close enough he gripped the trigger even tighter, hoping to delay death, to throw her off, but she found him, leaving him bloodied, sunk farther into the earth that had already half eaten him, his eyes still open. When Valentín Cobelo noticed the machine gun's silence, he raced toward it. As he approached, he saw General Larios, raised his machete high in the air, and charged. Larios didn't dare shoot but, instead, dodged out of the way. Valentín turned his horse to face Larios, standing firm. Their horses danced anxiously, side by side. Valentín suddenly found himself incapable of killing this man who hadn't wanted to kill him.

"Get out of here and take your men with you," he shouted.

"You haven't won yet!"

"Don't make me kill you!" Valentín drew closer to Larios.

"Just tell them you beat me. No one will ever hear of me again. Either get the hell out of here or kill me now!"

Francisco Larios searched deep within himself to find a spark of anger or cruelty that would allow him to pull the trigger. He had been ordered to kill Valentín Cobelo, but it wasn't enough. He had never imagined coming face-to-face with him in battle. He knew he could not bear to remember killing him for the rest of his life.

"I don't want to kill you, Valentín! You are not my enemy. I don't want you to kill me either, but I'm not afraid. Just get out of here! Neither of us wins by killing the other!" Francisco Larios put his gun back in his holster and turned his back.

They say that Francisco Larios killed him at Trescaminos. I heard it was a bloody battle, machetes everywhere, not even any bullets. They say that when Valentín Cobelo was about to kill him he stopped, like someone about to kill a friend. But they say he had no friends, that he was pure hate inside. Some say the next night he found out that his woman was back in Monreal and went looking for her. That's what I heard, but personally I think Francisco Larios got him there in Trescaminos.

THIRTEEN

ARMED AND FOLLOWING ORDERS, SEVEN OF VALENTIN Cobelo's men left the vast darkness of the desert and entered Monreal just before dawn. The streets were still black from the night before, and their steps made no sound in the thick night air. As daylight broke they cautiously approached Rosario Alomar's home. They kicked the door open and entered, yelling, "We're here to take you back, doña Rosario! General Cobelo sent us!"

Startled, the darkness scurried out of sight. A light illuminated the upstairs walls. Fortified with courage and motherly love, doña Severina confronted the men. Brushing aside her fear, she pointed an old shotgun at them and warned them that no one would take her daughter away ever again.

Not regarding her as a serious threat, but to ensure she

didn't get the wrong idea, they pulled their pistols out from under their serapes, the long barrels resembling snakes, and waited for her proud daughter to appear.

Dressed in black, her hair pulled back with a red ribbon, Rosario Alomar stepped in front of her mother. She looked down at each of Valentín Cobelo's emissaries. Only Julián Vela could look straight at her. Out of respect and admiration, he lowered his eyes.

Her fear having returned, now that she realized the inevitable, doña Severina dropped the shotgun and took her daughter in her arms, crying.

The pistols disappeared under the serapes.

Rosario hugged her mother and stared down at the men in the entryway. Then she gently pulled away from her mother and descended the stairs with confidence. "I knew Valentín would catch up with me sooner or later. You can be sure I'll run away from him again, from his damned desert, from all of you." She smiled proudly. "This is a curse we all must bear."

The men stepped aside to let Rosario pass. Her mother hurried down the stairs, crying quietly. Crushed, wishing she could offer her own life in place of her daughter's, she buried her face in her daughter's bosom. Rosario stroked her mother's hair as if she were a young girl, and then followed Julián Vela out of the house, the rest of the men falling in behind her. Julián placed Rosario behind him on his horse and gently nudged the animal into a gallop.

When her daughter had disappeared into the sunrise, doña Severina went back inside and collapsed onto a sofa. With her remaining strength she prayed to God that Valentín Cobelo be drawn into the depths of hell.

As they entered the desert, the men slowed their horses to a trot. Julián stopped. He took Rosario down off the horse and, without looking at her, tied her hands and said, "Forgive me. These are my orders, and I must obey."

Rosario looked at him boldly but without anger. Julián got back on his horse, tied the other end of the rope to his saddle, and urged his horse forward.

The sun was fully awake now and stood squarely in front of them. Its young heat rose up from the ground and the rocks and poured down from the sky, seeping into their bones, clutching at their throats. In a vain attempt to protect themselves, they closed their mouths and sweated. Rosario was bent over, her attention focused on the steps she never imagined she would have to take, watching her bare feet on the hot sand. She looked up every now and then to see the sun rising higher still in the sky. Soon it would fall straight down on her back. When her lips barely moved and her throat was as ragged as the endless terrain, she begged for water and fell to the ground, scratching and beating it, only to see Valentín Cobelo's face etched there.

Julián stopped and gave her water. The others drank too. He put his hat on her head and a serape on her back and helped her to her feet. They still had three hours to go.

When they arrived at La Higareda, the sun had scorched them to the marrow and they had run out of sweat. The horses were foaming, their sides heaving from exhaustion and dehydration, though they had been given most of the water on the trip.

The blinding white sun was perched at its zenith, sucking the color from the desert to use later, when it would paint the countryside a million shades of red. But that was still a long way off. Many hours remained before the sun and its stifling heat would fade.

Rosario's feet were bleeding and her lips were blistered.

She had no recollection of her final steps; they were blanked out, white, like the very center of the sun. Nor had she even noticed when one of the men killed a tarantula that was crawling on her petticoat.

Julián Vela told her they had arrived and laid her in the shade of Valentín's house.

None of the cobelistas at La Higareda spoke to the newly arrived men. Adelaida Morones and another woman offered them water and mescal. Then they ate some dried meat with broth and collapsed from exhaustion.

Julián Vela brought a wet salted cloth to Rosario and dabbed her lips with it. Although she seemed more dead than alive, he felt certain she would pull through. His experience in the desert had taught him what was bearable and what was not. He told her she would have to wait a few more hours until Valentín returned and decided what to do with her.

Watched closely by Julián Vela, the women wiped Rosario's feet with damp cloths. He leaned in to get a closer look. He had never seen feet so white and smooth, or toes so long and slender. He stared, tempted to touch them. Even in this condition she is amazing, he thought.

Cayetano Rosales, the old man, told them to take her inside. "This is bullshit!" he yelled. Julián Vela didn't dare carry her himself. He could not imagine holding her in his arms. The broiling sun was more than enough heat for him. He called over two men to help the women carry her into the house. All Julián could do was fan her with his hat.

One of the women left and returned with a cup of bean soup. Adelaida Morones spoke a few words to Rosario. "Why try so hard to get away when he's got you locked deep inside him?"

Rosario opened her eyes slightly and ate the soup they fed

her. Fragmented images, distorted memories unrelated to one another, haunted her. Now even her burning skin and aching, exhausted body seemed like a distant memory compared to those days she had spent waiting, body and soul twisted into knots, anxious to see General Valentín Cobelo again.

They say he loved her from the depths of his soul and with the strength of the earth and the sun and the wind. But their love was stronger than both of them. Well, someone told me that she was the one who loved him desperately; then she just stopped loving him and he went crazy without her. It was a cruel love, ravenous and devouring.

After resting indoors for a while, refreshed a bit by the damp cloths on her face, Rosario called for Julián Vela. "Where is Valentín?" Her voice was scratchy, diffuse. She licked her lips and had trouble swallowing. Her body was still burning hot and she was coughing.

"Don't upset yourself, doña Rosario. He'll be back soon; that's why he told me to bring you here. He'll come by dark, maybe before. Here, have some more soup."

His sympathy for her was mixed with a deep admiration. She had become a legend.

Submerged in a weakness that rendered her body useless, she could only feel her mouth and, now and then, her eyes. Wrapped in a blazing heat that surged from deep inside her, no longer caused by the retreating sun, Rosario Alomar knew that once again she was waiting for Valentín Cobelo to return. Her eagerness had died. The passion and uncertainty of those early days, his hands shaping her with his wild caresses, were no more. There was no more longing to be with him, wher-ever he went, no pride that he belonged to her.

He never told me he loved me. But I didn't want to say it to him either. I was afraid of loving him, letting myself be dragged around by it. How could I possibly tell him, now that he hates me, now that I fear him? There is no way anyone could still love after so much bloodshed.

A sharp pain stabbed at her chest. It rose up her neck, spreading to her ears and filling her head. She saw Valentín's face. He kissed her on the lips, trailed his mouth across her cheeks, her forehead, her eyelids, her nose, not hurrying, turning each kiss into a ritual. She tried to raise her arms and hands to caress him, but she couldn't reach him, she didn't have the strength.

"Don't let me die, Valentín."

"You're not going to die, doña Rosario, I promise. Don't think that."

Julián Vela dipped the cloth in the water and placed it on her forehead.

"Oye, Cayetano, look, la señora is going to die on us. I don't think she can take it. She's burning up with fever and she's coughing."

"She better not die for your sake. I hope the general gets here soon. I'll go tell the women to fix some herbs to lower the fever. You wait here."

"Julián? Julián! Where is Valentín? Has he gone to El Faro with Cipriano? I asked him to take me, but you know how he is. Lunch is going to burn. It's been on the fire too long. Just look at those pots boiling. Let's go get him. Will you come with me? I'm roasting in here. Look at the steam coming off those pots. I'm burning up, Valentín, I'm burning up!"

"Cayetano! Where are those herbs? Hurry the hell up!"

Rosario was no longer aware of the world around her. She had no idea that the noises, voices, and images that came to her were born from her delirium.

Shocked and frightened, Julián Vela looked at her with tenderness. He watched slow smiles spread across her face; unintelligible gestures moved her arms, peaceful sleep transformed into grimaces of panic and anguish. Her hair was soaking wet. Julián wiped her face and neck with the cloth, his hand trembling. Fear and desire made him lower the cloth to her firm breasts until she startled him, shouting, "He'll be back, Mamá, and I'll have to go with him. There's nothing else I can do. I have nothing other than my need to be with him. I'm afraid of him, but it's a fear that taunts me, lures me to the abyss. You have never seen his desert. I have and it burns me. His desert burns!"

"Calm yourself, doña Rosario, you're out of the sun now. Don't talk anymore. Just go to sleep now, please." Julián Vela cursed the hour he was told to bring her back.

"When is he going to be here? I don't want to wait anymore. Tell me, doña Castalia, when will he be back? I don't want to die before he returns. I'm not going to die now, am I, Mamá?"

That night, doña Severina heard someone knocking at her door. Weeping, aware of little beyond her grief, she thought that Rosario had returned.

"Rosario! Rosario!" She rushed to the door, opened it, and suddenly felt herself harden, then quickly soften again, drained and weakened. Life was playing a cruel joke on her. It was don Celestino Alomar.

"I didn't want to die alone," said the old man, sad-eyed

and wrinkled. He was like a wrecked ship, his once proud sails now sagging and empty. She moved aside to allow him to come ashore.

Begging God not to let Rosario Alomar die, Julián Vela spent the night trying to lower the fever that gripped the general's woman. Voices spoke to her, screaming at her from the desert. Her dead had come back. Julián couldn't distinguish among them. He didn't know about the sea and the man who had left her. When Valentín Cobelo arrived at daybreak with the rest of his men, Julián rushed up to him.

"La señora is dying, general, hurry."

Valentín rode slowly into La Higareda, not appearing to hear or see anything, not even turning to look at the man who walked next to him, his eyes full of tears. When he reached his house he dismounted and walked to the room where they were nursing Rosario. Adelaida Morones left them alone.

The men waited in the excruciating silence, sharing a sense of foreboding none of them dared mention. Their souls sensed the end of the story was near and they were not sure they wanted to take part in it. They did not know what it all meant, who this woman really was, even who the general was, this defeated man.

The door remained closed. Only the smell of sorrow escaped, a flash of clouded sunshine, a sour, dry taste in the mouth. The men were uneasy. Their hearts' insistent beating no longer afforded them the luxury of hiding behind a veil of indifference.

The women continued their chores, masking their thoughts, hiding the certainty of what was to come: that they would have to gather up their belongings and leave the desert. Not needing to talk to each other, they knew what would happen and felt sorry, not for themselves but for their men. Used to following, their men would soon have no one to lead them.

No one knew precisely what went on behind that door, what was concealed and protected. But no one really needed to know. All that could be known and all that mattered could be felt inside each of those present.

Cipriano, sitting on the ground next to Rarámuri, was as silent as the slow smoke rising from his cigarette. He was thinking about the past. There was nothing to look forward to.

Rarámuri threw his machete into the ground repeatedly, watching it cleave the earth and then pulling it out again, until suddenly he stood up and threw it far into the desert. He walked slowly toward it, not even looking where it had landed, gauging the distance in his mind.

"What is going on, Cipriano? This damned waiting is killing me." Julián Vela couldn't keep quiet any longer.

"Be patient, Julián, this story is almost over."

"What story? What the hell are you talking about?! Just look how few of us are left. *Mi general* has forgotten about us. He's even forgotten about himself. She's going to die, even I know that."

"It's between them, Julián. There's nothing we can do."

"What about us? Don't we matter anymore? We were loyal to him, Cipriano! We obeyed him!" Julián could no longer hold back his tears. "Is our general just going to abandon us?"

Cipriano looked at him with tenderness.

"Damned be the day I brought her back! Damn it, Cipriano! She was such a woman!"

Finally the door opened and Valentín Cobelo appeared with Rosario Alomar in his arms. Everyone stood still; all eyes were riveted on them. The women edged closer to their men, for protection. Valentín put Rosario on his horse and climbed up behind her.

"Where are you going, muchacho?" asked Cipriano.

"To be with her."

"What should I do with all this?"

"Just leave it. Let the desert have it."

Julián Vela ran behind them as they trotted off into the desert. "Don't go, General. Take me with you!"

Valentín Cobelo just looked at him, not stopping. He took off his gun belt and let it fall at Julián's feet. He dug his spurs deep into the sides of his horse, leaving behind his loyal followers, his men, and the women who followed them. Even Cipriano.

The houses are still there, in that place in the desert where the wind never stops blowing, shiny and warm during the day, cold and howling at night. Passersby sometimes take shelter there, but there is one door no one has been able to pry open. The other doors swing in the wind, banging against their frames all night, but that one door remains locked, inviolable, untouched, commanding respect.

No one ever saw Valentín Cobelo or Rosario Alomar again. They say a lamp burns in the house in Monreal, waiting for Rosario to return. They say maybe she never really existed. Maybe it was only a story.